FOR EVERY SIN

FOR EVERY SIN

Aharon Appelfeld

Weidenfeld and Nicolson
London

First published in Great Britain in 1989 by
George Weidenfeld & Nicolson Limited
91 Clapham High Street, London SW4 7TA

Copyright © Aharon Appelfeld 1989

Translated from the Hebrew by Jeffrey M. Green

British Library Cataloging in Publication Data
(applied for)

ISBN 0 297 79700 X

Printed in Great Britain by
Redwood Burn Limited, Trowbridge, Wiltshire

FOR EVERY SIN

I

WHEN THE WAR ENDED Theo resolved that he would make his way back home alone, in a straight line, without twists or turns. The distance to his home was great, hundreds of miles. Nevertheless it seemed to him he could see the route clearly. He knew that this would separate him from people, and that he would have to remain in uninhabited places for many days, but he was firm in his resolve: only following a straight course, without deviation. Thus, without saying good-bye to anyone, he set out.

He intended to advance slowly and stick scrupulously to the path, but his feet were avid for walking and wouldn't obey him. After about an hour he got tired and sat down. He was in an open, uncultivated field, with a few burned-out vehicles and food tins strewn about on it. These charred remains did not attract his notice. He wanted to rush forward, but fatigue halted his momentum and foiled him.

Now he took pains to walk in a straight line, at a uniform pace, restraining his feet. He was on a broad expanse that rose up above another plain, also broad. Far off some hills were visible, but other than that there was no sign of life. A dense silence clogged the air, leaving no room to spare.

Toward evening the landscape changed surprisingly. It was no longer a plain as he had imagined it but rather a valley surrounded by hills. A few trees rose up within it, tall and broad, reminding him of white birds. This was merely in appearance: the silence was total, there was not even one small bird. A dark blue sky dimmed overhead. He sat down and looked at it, and the more he looked, the more he felt his head growing heavy. "I have to shut my eyes," he said, shutting his eyes.

He calculated that so far he had covered three miles. He had deviated slightly from his course, but nothing that couldn't be corrected. From now on, if he was careful, he would not err again. That petty thought soothed his anger, and he opened his eyes.

Twilight came, quiet and restful. From the distant houses scattered about rose thin smoke. The sight aroused within him a strong desire for a bowl of soup, but he did not pursue that desire. He rose to his feet, looked for a stick and found one, and he immediately thrust it into the soft earth. That would be his sign. "I shall no longer stray from my course," he vowed to himself.

The sun was setting, and he strode on. It had been years since he had seen a sunset in the open. Sometimes, toward evening, a purple light would momentarily flood the camp assembly ground and be swallowed in darkness. Now the skies were open before him with a pure, tranquil blueness. The lights poured into him as into an empty vessel. For a while he sat without moving. When it got dark, he lay down on dry twigs and fell asleep.

He slept tranquilly and dreamlessly. The chill of the night seeped into his torn shoes, but he didn't wake up. He had become used to sleeping in bitter cold. Toward dawn he felt a pricking in his loins. He roused himself and got up. The stick, he found, was still standing in place, and he was happy for it as though for a familiar sign of life. Now he took calm, measured steps. From time to time he stopped, inspected the area, and stuck a stick in some elevated place. This strange business completely absorbed him, and he forgot that not long ago he had left the camp shed and his friends, and had fled.

Before long he was out of the plain and climbing. These were low hills from the crests of which one could view the entire valley. The valley was crisscrossed with paths and roads, but he set his course and did not stray.

From here he saw the refugees for the first time. They moved forward, scattered along the roads as though they were in no hurry. Several were sitting on their packs, others went down into gullies to rest. Theo reckoned that if he stuck to this course, he was liable to meet them. He had to correct his course, the sooner the better. The more he looked at them, the more he felt animosity flaring up inside him.

The lights grew dimmer and thick shadows, announcing rain, wandered across the hilltops. Theo wasn't afraid. The desire to distance himself from his brothers, the survivors, filled his body with strength. He turned north. In that area not a refugee was to be seen. Paths slid down the sloping hillside, and one could tell that no human foot had trod on them for months.

While he marched forward the sky opened and a full light, a compressed summer light, broke through from above. "I'm taking the right path," he said out loud for some reason. He took off his coat and spread it on the ground. For a moment he thought of lying down on the earth and closing his eyes, but he immediately recalled that the refugees were not far off, and if he wasn't careful, they might catch up with him.

He was still kneeling when, to his surprise, he noticed a chapel, standing at the foot of two tall oaks. That discovery pleased him. Roadside chapels had been among the most cherished secrets of his childhood, a memory from before memory. In the winters, while he was still a small boy, his mother used to take him to visit her mother in the country. His grandmother lived in a village, and the trip there, on a sled, took a full day. For hours the horses would gallop over snowy plains. Suddenly, out of the barren whiteness, a little chapel would rise, lit up with many candles, with two or three peasant women inside, kneeling beneath the icon and praying in muffled tones. His mother, in a broad winter coat, would get down from the sled carefully and stand at the entrance of the chapel. For a moment it seemed to the boy as though she too, a pretty woman, dressed in new clothing, was about to bend her knee and bow down next to the peasant women.

His mother had been charmed by anything precious and exquisite, but she truly venerated roadside chapels. On the way to her mother's she would often stop near a chapel and look at it for a long while. Her mother knew her weaknesses and would chastise her gently. "Don't worry, I'm not about to convert to Christianity," she would promise.

Theo veered off his course and descended to the small,

neglected chapel. Two emaciated hens stood guard at its entrance. As he approached they fluttered up into the branches. He wanted to go over and stroke them, but they screeched and squawked at him. A faded, smoke-stained icon stood within. Next to it, on a tray, bowls for offerings and two china candlesticks. A musty smell wafted from the building. He wanted to go inside, but the birds, sensing his intention, deafened him with their squawking.

For a long while he stood at the entrance to the chapel, and the longer he stood, the more his senses froze within him. Everything was forgotten. He tore himself away from the place. "If it starts raining, I'll come back here." The thought crossed his mind. He went back and climbed to the hilltop. He immediately discovered the poles he had stuck in the ground as he went, and they restored his confidence that indeed he had not strayed from his course.

He moved on without delaying. The sight of the chapel was gradually erased from his memory. Emptiness returned and filled it again. But suddenly a suspicion cropped up in his heart, that not far away the refugees were approaching him. Nothing was visible. The valley lay in utter repose, but nevertheless he decided that it would be better to go down and follow the stream than to encounter the refugees. They were definitely walking together, and they were liable to stray and come here. The suspicion urged him on, and he hurried down the hill.

Not until he was standing by the side of the stream was he calm. The quiet flow made him recall a forgotten melody. The melody flooded him, and he fell to his knees. The water was soft and fresh, and it immediately brought to his mouth the taste of the summery foods they used to serve in vacation homes. Now, for some reason, it seemed to him that it was not he who had sat in those very summer houses, but someone else, who had passed away in the meanwhile, and only the feeling of that person remained and rolled down to him.

Afterward he recovered his strength and marched on. Along the way he came upon cans of food, torn clothes, and a primus stove, but he didn't slow down. His own body heat was keeping him warm enough. Were it not for the rain, he wouldn't have stopped. A heavy rain surprised him and forced him to retreat to the hilltops. That retreat was useless. Not even the tall trees shielded him. The rain poured down angrily from the skies. So without realizing it, and with no alternative, he found himself among the refugees again, taking cover under a thin tent. The refugees were sitting quietly and withdrawn, not saying a word. A vacant stare shone in their eyes.

"Where are you from?" A man addressed him in a hollow, completely ordinary voice.

"Camp number eight," Theo answered directly.

"That was a good camp."

"Good, you say? How do you know?"

"I heard. In your place they distributed bread once a day. Isn't that so?"

"Vain rumors, let me assure you. No different from camp number nine."

Hearing these words, the eyes of the people sitting there started up, and they were angry at the questioner, seeking to silence him. The questioner felt that wordless flow and fell silent. In the middle of the tent stood an old army stove which did not give off a great deal of heat, but the window in its belly glowed red and gave a feeling of warmth. Next to the stove sat a few bundles and a pair of army shoes.

"Some coffee?" asked the man in that same unemphatic, dry voice, and without waiting for an answer he poured some in a mug for Theo. Theo took the cup cautiously. "In our place there were days when they didn't even give out a single slice of bread." The man spoke again, in the same voice with which he had begun. "In the last winter only water soup. Where are your comrades?"

"I don't know. Everyone went his own way," Theo answered quickly.

"We keep up our fellowship. Not many of us are left alive. If we did remain, that means we must stay together, right?" It appeared that he had expressed that idea more than once. The people sitting next to the stove didn't respond. "Most of our comrades died untimely, unseemly deaths," he added.

"Why did he say 'untimely, unseemly deaths'?" The thought crossed Theo's mind.

"And you separated? You didn't want to be together?" the man nagged.

"Yes," Theo answered curtly.

"Why did you scatter?"

"Because we didn't want to be together anymore."

That response made the tent even quieter. Theo thirstily sipped the coffee and the people observed his drinking intently.

"We decided to stick together. If we remained alive, that's a sign that fate wants us to be together. There aren't more than ten of us."

"And where are you heading?" Theo asked without noticing what he did, in the old way.

That question embarrassed the man. He turned for help to three of his comrades who were lit by the light of the stove, but help was slow in coming. Without assistance, then, he recovered and said, "We're heading for the Hungarian border. Most of us are from Transylvania. They also speak Romanian in our area. Where are you from?"

"From Baden-bei-Wien."

"From Baden-bei-Wien?" The man smiled. "All the rich Jews used to go to Baden-bei-Wien before the war. So your mother tongue is German. Strange, isn't it?"

"What's strange?"

"Strange to talk in the murderers' language."

"Not all the Germans are murderers." Theo surprised him. "You mustn't speak in generalizations."

"We, at any rate"—the man gathered his thoughts—"have encountered nothing but cruel taskmasters and murderers. We haven't found a single decent man among them."

"One mustn't generalize, in any case," Theo insisted.

"I don't agree. Murderers are murderers."

Now it seemed as if one of the men next to the stove was about to voice a comment. He merely appeared to be doing so. The man curled up in his coat, a faded army coat he had found in an abandoned storeroom.

"And where are you heading?" asked the first man in a more confident voice.

"Home."

"To Baden-bei-Wien?"

"Indeed."

That was the end of the conversation. One of the men sitting there handed him some biscuits, and Theo took them without thanking him. He was hungry. The longer he sat, the hungrier he became. For a moment he was about to say, "Don't you have anything to eat? My hunger is excruciating." But seeing their weary, expressionless faces, he stifled his request and said nothing. The daylight grew grayer, and cold air slipped through the slits in the tent.

After a long silence he asked, "Do you have any more biscuits?"

"We do. We have a whole box. Why didn't you ask? We also have coffee. Plenty of everything. It's hard to drag along these supplies. That's why we're stopping here."

"How long have you been here?"

"Since the liberation. It's hard to go far. It's easier for you. You're alone. And you don't have any supplies."

He almost said, "What do you need those supplies for?" But he immediately saw the stupidity of his question. The man caught the question anyway, and he answered, "You're right. Worldly goods bring worldly cares, as our fathers say, and they're correct. Since we found these supplies, we've been enslaved to them. If we had a wagon, things would be different."

The man was glad he had found the right words and kept mulling them over. Theo sat where he was and looked at him: about fifty; the war years had killed much of his will, but not his will to use familiar words again. He used them as though they hadn't become completely out of date. "It's easier for you. You're walking by yourself. You have no supplies." He fondled the words he had spoken before.

"You could also do the same thing." Theo couldn't contain himself any longer.

"True," said the man. "But we've sworn to each other that we'll never separate again."

"So why are you complaining?"

"I'm not complaining," said the man. "True, I also feel like getting up and going sometimes." The men around him didn't react to that statement, as though they realized it was only a vain wish. But that very statement aroused a kind of hidden guilt in Theo. He had abandoned his companions in suffering.

"Thanks," said Theo, rising to his feet.

"Where are you going in this rain?" The man addressed him the way one talks to a rebellious brother.

"I must," said Theo. For some reason he added, "It wasn't bad here."

"If that's what you want, I won't stand in your way. A man's wish is his honor," said the man, swallowing the saliva in his mouth.

Theo did not delay but went out into the rain. For a full hour he ran in the pouring rain. He spent the night in an abandoned barn, in the dry straw which blotted his drenched clothes dry. When he awoke the next morning his clothes were still damp but he was firm in his resolve to keep going. He had hardly left the barn when he felt that the contact with the refugees still clung to his clothing. He wanted to shake off that contact and the words that had stuck to him.

From here he could see the other part of the valley: a broad expanse that reminded him of a dried-up sea.

While he was surveying that area he noticed, to his surprise, that a guards' cabin stood at the foot of the hill. Cabins like these had been scattered around the camp. That discovery stirred some frozen fear within him, and he stopped where he was.

"I have to go up and see." He spoke in a voice that was not his own. But the fear was stronger than he, and he stumbled. That slight stumble immediately recalled to mind the faces of the refugees with whom he had spent a few hours, miserable faces, full of good intentions. "Don't go there," their voices warned him, but that voice he had used, full of fear and goodwill, made him stand strangely erect, and he picked up his feet and marched. From up close he could see a door, two windows, and, beside them, a water tank that towered over a scaffolding of planks.

He approached the door and knocked. The door of the cabin wasn't locked, and he opened it with ease. The sight that greeted his eyes astounded him with its neatness. Three iron beds, the mattresses wrapped with blankets. At the head of each bed was a folded blanket. A writing table made of planks. "This place was left in admirable order." The thought sped through his mind. A row of books lay on a long shelf, on another shelf were a breadbox, preserves, and a primus stove.

"Marvelous," he said, and he laid his body on one of the beds. Before long he fell asleep. In his sleep he floated on a green raft that whisked him through the water. At a distance on the shore he saw the refugees whom he had visited. They observed him with horror, as if he had taken leave of his senses. But Theo was pleased to be drawing away from them. The desire to be at a distance from them was stronger than any fear.

When he woke up it was already noon, quiet and easeful. No sound could be heard except for the creaking of the door, a comforting noise. "Where am I?" He tried to recall. The past few days and his purposeful walking had completely emptied his memory. He felt his legs. They were still asleep.

"I must get up," he said, and he was immediately surprised by the voice he produced. The silence had been total. What few sounds there were came from the wind scouring the two windows and the door. He rose and read the notice tacked to the wall. Standing orders, printed on thick paper that had yellowed. He read: "Length of watch, three hours. The guard will be dressed according to the season and fully armed. A soldier on watch will not speak with the other guards except in the course of his duties. The commander of the watch will be responsible for changing the guards and will be present at the changing of the guards." The language was clear and direct, and Theo smiled for a moment because he had been able to read and understand it. But he realized immediately: it was no wonder, for German was his mother tongue.

For some time he sat where he was and followed the rays of light flattening on the wooden floor in geometric shapes. Unaware of what he was doing, he calculated that the area of a parallelogram was equal to that of a square. The calculations took place in his mind of their own accord. He felt no effort.

"It isn't bad here. I could rest a little." In saying this he remembered the thirst that had plagued him for days and felt a craving again. He rose and walked to the door. The valley spread out in all its silent splendor. The shadows of the birches trembled noiselessly on the ground. The late-afternoon light was spread out, soft and warm, like a lap in which one can lay one's head.

He went to make a cup of coffee for himself. Everything was arranged in a corner: a jar full of coffee, cups, spoons, a box of matches. "While we were rotting in sheds, they sat here, drinking coffee and chatting." The thought passed through his mind. Within seconds the primus was roaring with a blue flame. The burner was polished, with neat holes, and it gave off thick heat. Minutes later the coffee was steaming. He extinguished the primus and sat at the table. The table was next to the window, looking out over a broad expanse, the entire valley, actually, as far as its narrow mouth. The isolated, scattered trees concealed nothing. The silence was full, not a sound was heard. "This is a comfortable place," he said again.

Later he took off his tattered clothes and stood naked in the cabin. That quick action, which he carried out without excess thought, frightened him for a moment. He covered his privates with a shirt. A pungent mustiness wafted up from the clothes. "To wash. The time has come for this body to wash," he chided himself, and with a sharp movement he skipped outside and opened the faucet of the water tank. It was the same kind of faucet he had in his home, made of nickel. The water was tepid. He closed his eyes, and a kind of feeling of relief, not devoid of pain, spread along his body. For a long time he stood beneath the water. An old song, a bawdy one, that they used to sing in little taverns not far from his house, suddenly hummed out loud in his mouth.

Undershirts and underpants were arranged in the cupboard, shirts and trousers. A homey smell of soap and naphthalene wafted up from the clothing. They happened to fit him. He stood up and strode in his new boots, and he immediately declared: "New boots." All at once the clean clothes gave him a strange kind of pleasure in life. Afterward he stood outside, and without feeling anything, he burned his clothes, the prisoner's clothing.

Then he got ready to take a turn outside, to survey the area and enjoy the sight of the evening. But he didn't do so. He sat on the bed. The evening lights quietly dripped into his soul.

He felt that his weak body, eaten up with hunger, which had not been in his possession for years, was now throbbing

in his chest. An old feeling of pleasure now flowed the length
of his legs. "Everything here is marvelously tidy," he stated
again. He got to his feet. The boots were made of thin leather,
and one could tell that the man who had worn them had been
careful to keep them looking good. The soles weren't thick,
but strong. He marched in place and marched again. That
action, which was intended merely to verify and ratify the
sturdiness of the boots, raised up within him, unnoticed, a
kind of alien and murky feeling. The feeling waxed within
him, and he said, "I'll stay here until I uproot all my weaknesses and fears. No one will have contempt for me anymore." Saying this, he felt he wasn't addressing the cruel
guards but his frightened brothers sitting in the tent, withdrawn and expressionless, serving him a cup of coffee and
biscuits with trembling hands. And when he knew that
clearly, he was even angrier, as though he finally understood
the source of that murky feeling.

II

AFTER SEVERAL DAYS of sitting idly, sleeping, and wandering about, he saw a woman approaching. From a distance she looked like a peasant, but her walk, an aimless gait, showed him his error. He got to his feet. The woman apparently hadn't noticed him and walked on. He stood and observed her tensely. Now it was clear to him beyond all doubt: one of the survivors.

"Hello," he called in a loud voice. "What are you doing here?"

The woman stood motionless.

"I asked what you're doing here," he called out again in the same loud voice. The woman ignored his call and continued walking. Now he saw her from close up: a tall woman, dressed in a prisoner's smock. Her eyes emitted a kind of sharpness. When she got close, he took a step backward and cried out, "Where are you from?"

"Camp number nine."

For a moment they looked at each other.

She asked, "Do you have anything to eat?"

"What?" The word slipped out of his mouth.

"I asked if you had anything to eat."

Without answering he turned his back on her and entered the cabin. First it seemed he was about to sit at the table, but he immediately got hold of himself, took two cans of food and a package of rusks and came outside. The woman was standing frozen in the same spot. "Take it," he said.

"Thanks," said the woman.

"You'd do well to get out of here," he said with a kind of forced quiet.

"Go to hell," said the woman and threw the food at his feet.

He went back into the cabin, sat by the window, and observed her. She sat where she was, not far from the cans she had thrown, with both arms around her knees. Even in that pose, horror was visible in her eyes, horror which had no more fear in it.

"What do you want from me?" He raised his voice and immediately regretted having said, "from me."

She moved her head without responding. He was going to shout, but his voice was blocked in his mouth. He walked out the door and approached her, saying, "What do you want?"

"Go away," she hissed.

"This is my place." Wickedness spoke from his throat.

She was wearing a prisoner's smock with a gray winter coat over it. The rips and patches showed that the garment had been tormented with her.

"My name is Theo." He tried to mollify her.

"I didn't ask."

He turned his back and set out. From this angle the broad, round valley looked sheltered within a band of green. He walked in a straight line and crossed the valley the long way. He remembered that the day before he had fallen asleep on the bed in his clothes, and in the middle of the night he had felt hungry but had been too lazy to get up and make a meal. Toward morning he had awakened in a panic, and afterward he remembered he had seen a woman in a dream.

He advanced. The valley proved to be wider than he imagined, surrounded by thickets and trees. The silence, flowing down from above, gathered as in pools. Years ago, when he was still a boy, his mother had taken him to the famous Heiml Woods. His mother didn't like dense woods, but she was drawn to the Heiml forest, perhaps because the trees there were short and lopped off on top, giving the place a sense of openness and abundance of light. They had spent a week in the inn, wandering about idly and eating berries and cream. At the end of the week his father had met them at the door, full of ire: "What will become of this boy? Because of his mother's frivolity he'll be stupid."

When he returned to the cabin it was already night. He lit the lantern and placed it on the cupboard. The flame lit the cabin and laid bare a corner he hadn't noticed before. Among other things were instruction manuals, propaganda brochures, a package of newspapers with holes in the sides, tied up with cord. The shelf was arranged nicely: a picture album, pebbles, and dried flowers sent from Munich. On a pink piece of paper was written: "From the rear to the front with love."

For a moment he wanted to get up and rattle the shelf, but

he didn't. He leaned over, picked up the splendid picture album, and cried out: "What cheap sentimentalism." That word, which he hadn't used in years, made him feel suddenly happy.

He opened a can of sardines, a carton of rusks, and a can of fruit and arranged them next to each other on the table. He immediately set to eating his meal. The sardines soaked in oil brought to his nostrils the scent of long rambles with his mother during the summer. His mother used to spread a cloth on the ground and they would sit and laugh out loud together.

Later someone knocked on the door. "Come in," he called out in a voice left over from former days.

It was the woman.

"What do you want?" he said, immediately wishing he could call the words back into his mouth.

The phosphorescence of her gaze struck him and he lowered his eyes.

The coat was big on her and the dirty striped smock hung down to her torn shoes. But her whole being, in the lamplight, bespoke frightening composure.

"Excuse me. My behavior was disgraceful." The word "disgraceful," which he hadn't used for years, summoned before his eyes an abandoned corner of his childhood, the backyard of his house.

The woman ignored his apology and asked, "What are you doing here?"

"Nothing. I'm taking a short break. I'm on my way home."

She tried to button her coat, but her fingers felt that the coat had no buttons. She gripped the lapels of the garment.

"What can I offer you?" he said, glad to find the right words. That direct, courteous address surprised the woman.

Her pursed mouth opened a little as though she realized the world was back to normal. Once again human beings offer you food and drink.

"What do you have to give me?" she said, the way she might have spoken to a waiter in a restaurant, but she recoiled immediately and said, "What difference does it make?"

"Sardines. There are plenty of sardines here."

"Thank you," she said. Now it seemed she was about to turn her back and go out. That was merely the way it appeared. She was weary and her arms sought support. She put out her arm and leaned on the wall.

"I can make you a cup of coffee."

"Coffee, gladly," she said with an old, homelike voice.

"I'm pleased," Theo said, rushing to the primus stove. She sat on one of the beds and followed his movements. "Everything a person needs is here. It's hard to get used to domestic things again." The woman didn't respond. She sank ever deeper behind her face.

"The coffee is good, the kind they used to sell at home. The very same box. How much sugar, please?"

"Two spoonfuls."

The preparations didn't take more than a few minutes. He placed a cup of coffee in her hands.

"Won't you have any?" she asked, domestically.

"I'll make some for myself soon. I have more than enough."

She drank without stirring it. He sat across from her, leaning over his cup. The primus stove still hissed. "It's been years since I've drunk a cup of coffee. This is a fine gift. I didn't even dream of it." She drank with moderate sips, the way one used to drink coffee in the afternoon on a balcony.

The shadow of a smile appeared on her tense face. "The coffee is excellent."

The evening lights slipped through the slats of the window and spread an old, forgotten, cozy feeling on the floor.

"What's your name?" he asked, as though he'd earned the right to ask.

"I?" she said, surprised. "My name is Mina."

"Mine is Theo."

She put the cup down on the table and looked around her, saying, "This is a spacious room." The movement and the words coming out of her mouth reminded him of a very familiar gesture, but he couldn't remember from where or when. In his mind everything was still jumbled. The friends with whom he had slept on a single platform in the labor camp returned to his memory from their journeys. His mind teemed like a railroad station. In truth he didn't want to see anyone, didn't want to talk, but the rain had done him in. It had held him up. Now this woman. It was hard to hear horror stories.

"What is this place?" she asked again, as if it weren't a military cabin but rather a cottage you rent at the seaside. Afterward she took off her coat and put it aside. Her prisoner's tunic was too long and gave her body surprising breadth. Her tense face grew round and she said, "An oasis. Coffee in the middle of the desert. Who could imagine such a rapid retreat? Such booty. In our camp people talked about twenty years of work. Suddenly it was all like a dream. You're yourself again, or at least it seems that way."

"I don't need anything. I intend to move forward without delay. I won't allow myself any more hindrances."

"Where do you intend to get to?"

"Home. Isn't that clear?"

His last words shook her body, as though he had not uttered everyday words but rather strange words with a frightening sound. Theo immediately added: "I decided to take the shortest path, to keep a distance from the refugees. The time has come to be by oneself a little bit, wouldn't you say so?"

"That's true," she agreed.

"The sight of the refugees drives me mad."

"What do you expect of them?" She surprised him.

"A quicker pace. That sitting on their bundles is an insult. There's a limit to humiliations. They mustn't sit on their bundles."

"What are they allowed to sit on?" She needled him for some reason.

"On anything, but not on their bundles."

His voice had an unpleasant sharpness. Mina grasped the cup and bent her head, as though seeking to soften his rage somewhat. Theo got up and put out the primus stove, and the silence of the night enveloped the cabin on all sides.

"Where are you from, if I may ask?" Mina broke the silence.

"From Baden-bei-Wien."

"Interesting. Me too, from not far from there, a very small town, Heimstadt. I doubt you've heard of it."

"I have. I've even been there once. My mother took me to see the stocks in the town square."

"I thought no one had ever heard of that obscure place."

"My mother took me everywhere where there was something unusual. She knew Austria like the back of her hand."

Mina chuckled. Her laughter revealed a very familiar feature in her face. From when and where, he couldn't remember. He wanted to ask her for details, but his mouth was sealed. The more he sat, the more it was shut tight.

Mina, for her part, praised the cigarettes he offered her. "Years without cigarettes destroyed the image of humanity within us. I knew a very strong woman who took her own life because she couldn't stand that suffering any longer. As long as she had cigarettes, she was in high spirits and encouraged others, but the moment they ran out, she sank into melancholy. Before her death she said, 'Without cigarettes there's no point to life and the best thing is to clear out of here before it's too late.' "

"I overcame that weakness."

"I'm lost without cigarettes," Mina said with a trembling voice. "Most of my thoughts, all during the war, were bent on cigarettes. That's shameful, but it's the truth. There were days when I gave up a portion of bread for a cigarette."

"In our camp there was solidarity. We divided everything equally."

"In our camp people stole like animals. I can't forgive myself. What could I do? I'm lost without cigarettes."

Now her eyes began to concentrate on a single point. Theo sat by her side and looked at her tensely. Suddenly, without saying a word, she sank down and fell asleep. Theo took two blankets from the heads of the beds and covered her.

The next morning the sky was clear, and no wind blew through the trees. The valley bathed in its full greenness, but from where he was standing it looked narrow for some reason, pressed between steep hills. Now he remembered Mina's arrival clearly. From the moment she came in he knew that a kindred spirit was at his side, but her eyes had emitted a kind of sharp horror, and he withdrew. Later he wanted to ask her

about a few things that had happened to him on his way
there. He wanted to ask her about the abandoned chapel he
had found at the foot of the mountain.

When he came back from his morning stroll she was still
sleeping. In the meantime he got the primus stove ready,
opened a can of sardines, added some rusks and dried fruit,
and placed it all on the table. A person could stay here for a
whole year, eating and drinking. They prepared everything
with precision and order. You can learn something from
them. Yes, you can. Even from the way they had left the place
you can learn something. Without panic. Everything in its
place.

When Mina awoke he immediately offered her a cup of
coffee. The sharpness of her eyes waned slightly. Other lines,
softer ones, crossed her face. She sat up on the bed and lit a
cigarette. "A cup of coffee and a cigarette. Who imagined
such gifts? We've already been in the world of truth, and
we've come back from there. It's interesting to come back
from there, isn't it?"

"In our place, in camp number eight, they didn't talk
about death." He made his voice stiffer.

"They didn't talk about it in our camp either, but it was
with us all the time. We got used to it. Now I'm a little
frightened."

"Why?"

"I don't know. Last night I dreamed about the other women
in my shed. Why did I set out by myself?"

"A person has to be by himself a little bit. We weren't born
in a flock. Togetherness drives me out of my mind."

"The other women in my shed were good to me. We
helped each other."

"Now the time has come to separate. This being together weakens us. One mustn't be together. A man in the field is brave. But with others he's swept along like a beast. We mustn't be together. Everyone for himself. In that way you can also maintain your inner order. This room, for example, shows inner order. They retreated calmly. They left everything in its place. It seems to me that we should respect that. You have to say a few words in praise of precision and order."

"I," said Mina, "am not so tidy. In all my school report cards it said, 'Not Orderly.' "

"I wasn't particularly orderly either. But now I'm going to try very hard. I won't give in to myself."

"It doesn't look as if I'll change," she said.

Afterward they sat without saying anything. The morning lights flowed inside and brought with them a kind of refreshing pleasantness. For a moment Theo wanted to tell her about everything that had happened to him on the way there, the sights and the chapel, but he controlled himself. Part of his inner self still slept, and another part of it teemed with wanderlust. One mustn't draw close to people. In the end people don't do any good for each other. Who knows what secrets she bears within her? He kept his peace and revealed nothing to her.

Later he went over to the map on the wall and, with a kind of military precision, showed her the nature of his route, the valleys, the mountains, and the rivers that stood in his way. The refugees also had to be taken into account. They were scattered on the hilltops. In the end he reckoned and found that the distance to his house did not exceed five hundred miles—that is, two months of walking.

"I'm afraid to go home."

"What are you afraid of?"

"All the people dear to me are no longer living."

"How do you know?"

"I heard."

"I decided not to be afraid."

"You're doing the right thing. Fear is a contemptible emotion. It should be uprooted. You're right, but it doesn't look as if I'll ever change."

The days were bright and chilly, and Mina didn't get out of bed. They ate fruit compote from the can and drank coffee. It was hard to coax complete sentences out of her. She drowsed without asking a question or making a complaint. "Why won't you eat some rusks?" he implored her. The words remained suspended in the air. Mina was drowning in a long sleep which grew longer daily. Fatigue also tried to cling to him, but he decided: I will only sleep in moderation. Prolonged sleep is a disgraceful surrender.

Now his day was divided in a strange fashion, wandering in the valley, waiting for Mina to awaken, and careful inspection of the military map that was hanging on the wall. The route was marked on the map, a dotted pencil line to Baden-bei-Wien. The thought that if he started on his way at once, he would be home in two months, made him impatient.

For the past few days, to tell the truth, he had intended to leave her and set out. But for some reason he didn't do so. Perhaps because he hoped she would free him of that obligation. He would sit by her bed and contemplate her sleep. Her sleep was deep, as though she were becoming attached to the inanimate objects around her.

Finally he took courage, folded the map, put an army blanket on his shoulders, and set forth. The light was full.

The rain that had fallen at night had seeped into the ground and been soaked up without leaving puddles. He crossed the valley with a broad, firm stride. At the first lookout point he stopped and spread out the map, immediately identifying places. It was a regular army map, quite accurate. The identifications pleased him. The course was plain to see, and for three miles there were no hidden areas. Not only that, the low vegetation and the rocks scattered densely indicated, more than any identification on the map, that the land was uninhabited, and during the war it had apparently been completely forgotten.

After marching for three hours, he sat down. The weariness that had been hidden within him took over his legs. Now, somehow, it seemed to him that he had not followed his course to this place, that he had strayed and gone out of his way. Two miles ahead rose a wooden building with two chimneys. The building was indicated on the map. He prepared to get up and set out for the building, but night fell all at once and bound him to his spot. For a long time he sat and looked at the darkness. The darkness grew steadily thicker, and before long it was absolute.

He curled up in the blanket and shut his eyes. The course which he had marked on the map was now stamped onto his brain, strong and bright. As if it were not a course strewn with obstacles but rather a smooth track on which cars glided as though by themselves. The twists and turns were indeed many, but the track was smooth and the cars skimmed along easily. Theo was glad for a moment to see the cars moving, but suddenly they slowed down and halted. The recoil and the stop broke the track, and the wide gates of sleep opened before him.

Now he saw his mother. She was approaching him with

quick, firm steps. "Mama, I've been looking for you for years," he told her in an everyday voice.

"And I was waiting for you in Hofheim," she said, not speaking overly emphatically, as though it were a matter of a small misunderstanding.

"And I've been waiting for you here."

"What a silly mistake I made. I'm always causing mix-ups. Where did you get those clothes? Aren't they army clothes?"

"I found them in a cabin. The blanket, too."

"The nightmare has finally passed, my dear."

The cold awakened him, and he stood up. The short meeting with his mother in the railroad station of Baden-bei-Wien filled him with dread. It had been years since he'd seen her in summer clothes. She would often stay with him in his sleep, sometimes a whole night, but never so easily. For a moment he was glad he had abandoned the cabin and started on his way. If he hadn't left, he wouldn't have met her. Any delay was sinful. From now on, only his route. Without any deviations or compromises.

As he stood, his spirits fell. There was no apparent reason for it. The morning light was full, the countryside spread out before him, the map was accurate, and his will was also strong, but something within him told him not to advance anymore but to return to his point of departure. Without the correct point of departure, there is no progress. For a moment he wanted to deny that feeling, but thirst conquered him.

He desired nothing but a cup of coffee. All his senses were concentrated on that desire. If a hand had offered him a cup of coffee, he would have calmed down and stayed where he was, but no hand offered, and he stood up and returned to where he had started.

He moved slowly, void of all thought, along the green

valley he knew like the back of his hand. He did what he had to without any pleasure. At noon he stood at the door of the cabin. Mina, to his surprise, was awake and sitting on the bed. "I'll make a cup of coffee," he said as if nothing had happened.

"You're good to me," said Mina.

"Why do you say so?"

"You're good to me," she repeated, and it was clear she had no more words in her mouth. Theo was struck with fear. For a moment it seemed to him that his mother's voice accompanied her. He lit the primus stove and the noise deafened him.

Later he spoke, out of any context, of the need to overcome weakness and fear and set out on long journeys, to breathe mountain air and drink flowing water, and, mainly, not to be together with others anymore. Mina felt the suppressed anger in his voice, but she didn't know what to say to him. The fluids she was drinking weakened her even more, but she still said: "You're good to me, more than you need to be," and she fell asleep.

From then on she didn't leave her bed. If she slept too long he would wake her and feed her a few spoonfuls of liquid. The days passed with no change. Sometimes thirst for the open road would awaken within him and draw him outside. But he didn't go far. The rain kept falling at night, and in the daytime the sky was clear. He calculated and found that if he made an effort he would get home in the spring. One evening she woke up and said, "Why are you delaying because of me?"

"I'm doing it willingly."

"A person must take care of himself." Her voice had returned to her.

"There's time. It's still raining anyway."

"You have to get home in time. What did you study?"

"I was just beginning German literature, first year."

"You can still manage to register for the second semester. It's too bad to lose more time. You've lost enough."

"It doesn't matter."

"It does matter," she insisted. "A person must finish his studies. Don't delay." She immediately fell back down and sank into sleep. He knew: it was not she who had been speaking, but a voice remaining within her from bygone days; still her delirious words made an impression on him. Now he remembered his first contact with the university, the fear and formality that had seized him upon seeing the old building.

Afterward she slept for two straight days. In vain he tried to awaken her. She was imprisoned in sleep. For a moment it seemed to him that if he sat by her side he too would sink into sleep. Heavy fatigue seeped into his limbs and drew him toward the bed. "I mustn't sleep," he called out loudly.

"I'm getting right up." She awakened in a panic. Now he saw clearly: a few of his mother's beautiful features were on her face. There was also some similarity in her expression.

"You have to drink." He tried to soften his voice.

"Isn't there any bandage here?" she asked in a domestic tone.

"There's a box full of bandages." He was glad he could come to her aid.

She pulled up her prisoner's smock and two wounds the size of fists suppurated in her thighs. Theo looked at them for a moment and froze.

"The women in the shed told me the wounds would heal. There was nothing to be afraid of. It's from the cold." She spoke in a frighteningly practical way. She apparently expected Theo to agree, but Theo was speechless, all words were cut off in his mouth. Finally he said, "You have to rest. You can't travel."

"I'll walk slowly," she said, mostly to appease him.

"You have to see a doctor. Those are big wounds."

"The women in the shed told me that fresh milk and vegetables cure wounds like that. Don't delay on my account. You have to get to the university and register in time. You mustn't miss registration. I'll move on slowly until I get to a village. In a village there will be fresh milk and vegetables."

"No, you mustn't move. I'll bring some." He commanded her the way one speaks to a prisoner.

"Pardon me," said Mina. "I beg your pardon."

"I'll bring milk and vegetables. If there's a doctor I'll bring him with me."

"Don't bother. Everyone has to take care of himself. You have to register. You've lost three full years. You should be in the last stages now. I'll walk slowly. I'll stay in the village for a month or two. The country food will cure me, and then I'll return home."

"We aren't like beasts." He spoke succinctly and sharply.

After bandaging her wounds she got out of bed and sat next to the screened windows. Her face was transparent and a kind of softness flowed from it. Theo's tongue was in a hurry to speak, and he talked of the necessity of eating fresh food, fruit and vegetable juices. He spoke with the old kind of emphasis, the way they used to talk before the war. But his tone was heavy and firm. Mina opened her eyes in fear. Theo did not feel at ease until he cried out: "There can be no life without fresh juice."

"Excuse me for showing you the wounds. I made a mistake. I beg your pardon."

"A person must show others"—he spoke with a strange sort of authority—"and demand help. A person who makes no demands and isn't obstinate will never achieve anything. I, at any rate, intend to go to the village and bring back fresh food. I'm tired of canned food."

"Don't trouble for me."

That request merely stirred up a confined stream of words within him. He spoke of the need to live a full and proud life. A person who doesn't live a full and proud life is like an insect. The Jews had never taught their children how to live, to struggle, to demand their due; in times of need, to unsheathe the sword and stand face to face against evil. The wicked had to know that people weren't afraid either of cold or of death. They had the courage to stand fast and not fear.

Mina managed to go back to bed on her own. The many sharp words that had left Theo's mouth made her shrink. She lowered her head to the folded blankets and closed her eyes.

At night she woke up and Theo helped her get out of bed. Her face was bright, and she spoke softly of the need to become active again. Clearly talk was beyond her strength, but she forced herself. Theo was sunk into himself and might not have heard. He, at any rate, promised her that as soon as the morning dawned he would set out for the village to bring her fresh food. The canned food was poisonous, and she was urgently in need of fresh vegetables. Mina trembled. "Don't delay because of me. I'll manage. People have always helped me. I don't know if I'm worthy of them." Later she added, "I feel better. I can set out easily."

"I'm going at dawn, and I'll come back in the evening. The distance from here to the village is four miles. I can easily manage that."

"I feel better, and I'm very grateful to you for all your

assistance. You can go on without any concern." Those reassuring words made him suspect that Mina was tricking him, but he ignored the suspicion. A powerful desire throbbed in his legs and drew him outdoors.

At first light he was already crossing the valley. No thought at all was in his brain, only a strong drive to swallow the distance. He advanced with the same urgency as when he had left the refugees and set out on his course. After walking for two hours he climbed to the top of a hill. The area was hilly, covered with low trees. A kind of hesitation crept into his heart and delayed him. But, as before, he commanded his legs to move, and they indeed moved on.

For many hours he walked without straying. On the hilltops there was no change: low hills, rocks, and clearings, an expanse with no paths and no human voice.

Toward evening he spread the map out on the ground and immediately he realized he had erred. He had taken the right course, but he hadn't estimated the distance correctly. The distance to the village proved to be seventeen miles, not four. Not only that, two rivers were marked on the map.

The light grew dimmer and he sat down. Fear bound him to the spot. If the light had persisted, he would have risked going back. But the evening was fading fast. The horizon was covered with thick specks of darkness. He saw Mina's wide-open eyes with a kind of transparent clarity. Suffering had not blemished them.

Only now did he understand what he hadn't understood before, that she had indeed released him from all obligation. But for his part he ought not to have accepted that from her. There are obligations which one mustn't evade. True, the evasion wasn't absolute. He had set out for the village to fetch vegetables. But because of his hesitations everything had gone wrong, and he was doubtful whether it could be set right.

When the dawn broke he saw how thick the vegetation was, the visibility was poor, and the hill was steep, with no steps. Go back, he ordered his legs, and they set out.

First he tried to return by the roundabout route he remembered, but he immediately decided he must take a straight path, cutting across the hilltop. The many thoughts scurrying about in his brain gradually evaporated. The drive to return to the valley completely filled him.

The shortcut, he found, was not shorter. It seemed to him he was getting farther and farther away. The dim morning lights made him think of the labor camp and the shouting of the prisoners, whom the Ukrainian guards used to beat at the exit gate. The thought that he was liable to go back to the camp didn't frighten him.

Only later, by chance, did he discover the valley at his feet. The discovery inspired his feet with new power. In a few minutes he was down below. At that point the valley was deeper than he imagined. He advanced slowly. Tension and fatigue flooded him and left a kind of weakness within him. For a moment he wanted to sit and lean on the trunk of an oak. He had barely sat down when, as if through a thin pane of glass, he imagined he saw Mina. Resignation marked her face. How few were the words he had exchanged with her— just isolated syllables. Now was the time for heart-to-heart conversations. It was good to be with people who had been in the camps, to listen to their voices and drink coffee with them. Mina had been in the camp from the moment it had been established. He should make her good meals and watch over her.

When he knocked at the door of the cabin he expected, for some reason, to hear, "Come in." No voice answered. He knocked again and waited. When he finally opened the door he saw that everything was in place, and Mina was gone. He went up very close to her bed, returned to the door. The cans of food were arranged in the same order, even the shelves with the booklets. He lay on the bed and said, "That's that."

III

LATER HE CALLED, "Mina," as if she were sitting outside. His voice returned to him, cut short, and with no resonance. The cabin was silent and orderly, as he had seen it at first, which somewhat quieted his fear for a moment. She had certainly gone out for a walk; he used a sentence from past days. He immediately went over to the primus stove to make himself a cup of coffee.

The coffee and the cigarettes thawed the muscles of his legs, and he sat by the table. A few green spots fluttered before his eyes and melted away without leaving any feeling in him. For a moment it seemed to him that he was not the same man who had returned but rather part of him. A segment of himself remained hanging on the hilltops and would return here in time. Theo raised his head and looked out through the screened window, as though seeking that part of his being which had remained in the hills.

For a long while he sat, gradually sipping the light and tasting a kind of familiar bitterness with every sip. At noon he went out and called out, "Mina." His voice echoed this time and returned to him stronger than his voice. No answer came. A bright sun stood in the heavens and struck the damp earth with its hard rays. A few birds stood on the bare branches, without a chirp.

Only later did he remember that he had meant to get to the village. A kind of repressed grudge that had been oppressing his chest broke out in a short groan and was halted. If someone had offered him another cup of coffee, he would have thanked him very much.

"Why did she go away without waiting for me?" Anger passed over his lips. But he immediately grasped that the woman, with those wounds in her thighs, couldn't walk very far. He should go out right away, while there was still light, and look for her in the surrounding area. She was certainly sitting in a hollow waiting for him. That practical thought roused him to his feet, but it did not bring him outside. He lit a cigarette and prepared himself a cup of coffee. The thought that the supply of coffee and cigarettes was good for many months pleased him in the most selfish way.

Now he felt like going out to the fields and shouting out loud: "Mina, Mina," but he decided not to do that. Rather he would head in the direction where he had first met her. For some reason he was sure he would find her there. He stood up and spoke the following sentences: "What made you go out, Mina? Didn't you know I would return soon?" He walked about the place without saying anything, but nothing moved. In the distance he heard a few explosions. They were faint, without any breath of danger. Afterward, he nevertheless called, "Mina, Mina," as if to do his duty. His legs drew him back to the cabin, and he returned.

Evening fell now, tranquil and silent. The cool, transparent lights sprawled on the windowsill and gave it the look of the window at home. He lit the primus stove. The blue flame made its old, familiar humming sound.

He drank the coffee and lit a cigarette and tried to recall how he had lost his way. But, maddeningly, he couldn't remember a thing. On the contrary, it seemed to him he had taken the right way, and if he had gone on, he would have gotten there. Unaware of what he was doing, he read the standing orders that hung on the wall. There were a few military terms he didn't understand, and he tried to guess their meaning.

The suppressed anger returned, surprising him. He remembered the refugees who had delayed him on his way. Their faces looked flushed from sitting by the stove so long. "Get outside. Sitting by stoves makes your face ugly. You have to go out and work or run, not sit next to stoves. Anyone found sitting next to stoves will be ostracized." Strange, it had been years since he'd heard the word "ostracized." All during the war they hadn't used that word. Now, it had come out of hiding, as it were, and presented itself naked. For a long while he stood on the threshold of the cabin without movement. A few words raced about in his brain. He remembered some of them and was pleased to greet them. Still, he was weary from the day and from standing, and without further thought he went to bed, curled up, and fell right asleep.

When he awoke the light was already prostrate in the window. He sat up in bed. Mina's absence only disturbed him superficially, as though it were a question of some small misunderstanding which would soon be resolved. In the labor camp people would fight over a piece of bread at night and part forever the next day. Sadness was as though abolished from the heart, leaving only a strong feeling, fed by hunger, that this life, cruel and temporary, would finally cast anchor in another region. Strangely, that feeling didn't make the people any better. People fought avidly and angrily over every scrap of food and every scrap of free space. Now he saw their faces with a kind of cold clarity: faces that knew the shame of suffering but were not refined, only coarse and blemished. Now too he knew that one mustn't reproach them, but nevertheless he couldn't overcome the repugnance that surged up within him. They let her go away. She had deep wounds in her legs. "Why did you harm her?" he raged. As though she weren't one of them but taken prisoner by them.

Afterward his memory gradually emptied out. He felt it emptying out. His temples pressed in, and his eyes seemingly closed by themselves. Fear gripped him. It seemed to him that he would never see his mother's beloved face again. He put out his hands and touched his feet. His feet stood firmly on the ground. That firmness pleased him, and he opened his eyes.

For some reason he headed south. The light that had greeted him on his arrival there now flowed thickly and with great abundance. The thin shadows were scattered along the valley to its rim. The hillcrests rose, naked and empty.

For a long while he walked. The farther south he got, the stronger grew the feeling within him, that once again he was walking on the straight course he had seen with such a thirst from the camp, a broad course, empty of people, which would bring him straight and easily, as though by river, to his home.

That, it turned out, was merely an illusion.

"Do you have a cigarette?" A voice startled him.

"What?" He was frightened by the call.

"I'm asking for a cigarette."

At his feet a man of about forty was sprawled, still wearing a prisoner's uniform, with his mouth open, an uncouth smile pushed back on his lips.

"I do," Theo answered, quickly handing him a cigarette.

The man brought the cigarette to his mouth and said, "Heartfelt thanks. I am ashamed of myself. This dependence on cigarettes is my damnation. I don't know how to overcome it. I would give up anything. I don't need food or drink. I can't give up cigarettes. That's a dreadful weakness. A disgrace that words can't describe."

"What are you doing here?" asked Theo, impolitely.

"Nothing." As he said so, his smile became even more uncouth.

"Where are the other prisoners from your shed?"

"They headed east. It was hard for me to bear their happiness, their satisfaction. I, at any rate, intend to remain here. Perhaps some change will take place within me."

"Isn't the loneliness hard for you?"

"There's no loneliness here. People hungry for life surround you everywhere. I hate people hungry for life. That avidity is uglier than any disfigurement. But what can I do? I have no choice. I'm addicted to cigarettes. Here, despite everything, you find a butt, somebody gives you one, or you steal."

Theo fell to his knees and gave the man a light. The man took a few puffs, looked at the cigarette with eyes full of desire, and said, "The very best kind." In his look there was neither pain nor sadness, but rather a kind of sharp transparency, a strong pallor, freckled with a few spots on his skin.

While they still stayed facing each other, a few dark sobs sliced through the silent air.

"Who's shouting?" asked Theo out loud.

"They're beating the traitors and informers. Didn't you hear?" A malicious smile spread on the man's face, making its ugliness complete.

"Why are you pleased?"

"I?"

"Your face, at any rate, showed malicious pleasure."

The man's lips changed expression and took on a disgusted mien. "I won't ask you for anything. There's something bad in you."

"Why are you saying that to me?" Theo stepped back a little.

"I'm saying what I feel. The time has come to tell the truth. All those years I restrained myself."

"What truth are you talking about?"

"About people's nothingness, their stinginess, their foolishness, and their malice."

"Am I stingy? I gave you a cigarette."

"Thank you. You didn't give generously. I had to ask you."

"I don't understand."

"Don't play the innocent. You know just what I mean. I despise miserly people."

"What should I have done?"

"Not waited. Offered with a generous hand. Now do you understand?"

Theo intended to answer him, but he didn't. He continued walking. Refugees surrounded the mountain on all sides.

They lay beneath the low trees, quiet and gaping. From here he could see parts of their faces, their bare feet, and their bruises.

He considered heading for the hilltops beyond and getting away from them, but he immediately understood that he couldn't do that, that he had to free Mina first. The thought occurred to him that now Mina was imprisoned in one of the tents, surrounded by people feeding her sardines and drilling it into her that she had to be with everyone, that in every generation the Jews were together, and now too they must not abandon the community. That thought struck him with horror—he raised his voice, but voicelessly he cried out, "Set Mina free. Let her go free."

Now Theo remembered the man's pale face with a kind of painful clarity, as he pierced him with his eyes and wounded him. For a moment he wanted to double back to the man, to make him see his error and to rebuke him, but he immediately thought better of it and continued on in the way he was going.

Later he thought of returning to the cabin, of lighting the primus stove, and making himself a cup of coffee. The thought that he had left the cabin open and untended panicked him into motion. That was a mere momentary twitch. He remembered that he had come here to look for Mina, and until he found her he would not return to the cabin. He took off his hat and lit a cigarette, feeling easier right away.

"I'm looking for a woman named Mina." He addressed one of the refugees lying there, a man of about fifty, still wearing prisoner's clothes.

"Who are you looking for?" the man said, absentmindedly.

Theo realized that his question had been fruitless and was

about to turn aside. Still, he made an effort and called out Mina's name, like someone prepared to do anything, even humiliate himself.

"I've never heard of her," said the man impatiently.

Theo understood explicitly that he had been mistaken in addressing him, and he didn't try to set things right anymore. But the man seemed to regain his self-possession and said with strange seriousness: "It does no good to search. Why deceive yourself?"

"Why are you telling me this?" Theo spoke to him softly, but bitterly.

"Because it will do no good to search," the man insisted.

"How can you be so sure when I'm talking about a woman whom I saw just yesterday? I talked with her and drank a cup of coffee with her."

"If that's the case, I beg your pardon," said the man, not so much acknowledging his error as wishing to get rid of him.

"I went out looking for fresh food in the village, and when I came back I didn't find her," Theo tried to explain.

"You'll certainly find her. There are lots of refugees down below."

"The trouble is, I don't know her family name."

"You certainly remember her face."

Theo looked at the man as though he were trying to plunder his last remnant of hope, but the truth was even more bitter. Mina's face had drifted from his memory, and he doubted he would recognize her in that pile of refugees, so similar to each other, and not only in their dress.

"Down below there are lots of refugees," the man called out loud, as if Theo had already gone away. Theo stood still.

The silence all around was complete. The refugees scattered on the hilltops didn't make any noise at all. But below, in a declivity like a crucible, a mass of refugees raced about. From here they looked short and lively, ants tangled up with each other, with no way out.

"I have no desire to be among them again." Theo unintentionally revealed his secret.

"I wouldn't go down there either, for all the money in the world." The man used an expression from bygone days.

"Why?" Theo tested him.

"Because they remind me of the labor camps," said the man simply.

"And you intend to stay here forever?"

"I'm better off hungry than in their company. Here at least there's no noise. The noise drives me out of my mind."

Theo understood his meaning very well, or rather his feeling, because a similar feeling also dwelt within him.

"Who is the woman you're looking for?" The man softened his voice somewhat.

"I met her a few days ago." Theo spoke blankly, without providing any details.

"Don't worry. You'll find her. You're still young. You have years ahead of you."

"I'm worried nevertheless," said Theo. A cold wind penetrated his shirt, and he said: "It's cold today, isn't it."

The stranger looked up and said, "I'm not cold yet."

Theo knew just what the word "yet" hinted at when the other man used it, and he also knew that it bore no trace of arrogance or of trying to make an impression, but nevertheless there was something threatening in the sound of that word, and he walked away. Again he stood on a hilltop. Weariness fell upon him, but he wasn't hungry. The scraps of bread and sausage scattered on the ground only disgusted him; it was evident that the people who had sat here some time ago had also been disgusted by the food.

"I'm going back to the cabin. There's no point to this running around. Otherwise someone will grab the cabin, and I won't have anything. Not a cup of coffee, not a pack of cigarettes. In the cabin I have everything." The words passed through his brain, and he felt thirsty. The thirst sped his feet, and he took several steps. But his feet, as though in a dream, were heavy and shackled down.

While he stood there a young woman approached him and said, "Would you happen to have a cigarette? You frightened me. I thought you were a German soldier."

"This is booty," said Theo and immediately was sorry he had used that word.

"I have more than enough food, but I don't have any cigarettes."

All the years of the war were stamped into her youth. But a few thin and delicate lines peeped through the puffiness, and one could tell that the girl came from a good home, had studied in high school, and that her parents had loved her and been proud of her. That discovery pleased him, and he chuckled.

"Why are you laughing?" The girl was surprised.

"I remembered something."

"What, if I may ask?"

"I remembered high school."

"I was in my last year. The war broke out in the middle of my matriculation examinations, and now I have no diploma."

"You have nothing to worry about. You can always make it up." The words were ready in his mouth.

"I've forgotten everything. I have no concept anymore. Once I was excellent in mathematics and Latin, and now it seems to me as if I never studied a thing."

"That's just an impression."

"I hope so. I have a desire to study. I always was a devoted student." The girl was dressed in tatters, and her swollen, unwashed face expressed a kind of pained, youthful surprise, as though she had been caught out of place. "I intend to continue my studies. I hope they'll take the war years into consideration."

"That goes without saying. That's the regulation." Surprisingly, his lost civilian language came back.

"They'll understand?" the girl wondered. "Are you sure?"

"I'm sure," he said.

"Excuse me," she said.

Not far away, in a puddle, an informer wallowed and begged for his life. Two men, not young, stood over him, holding boards. "I also lost everybody, have pity on me," he begged, trying to remove the mud that stuck to his face. The people lying about didn't meddle in this act of retribution. "Have pity on me." The beaten man addressed the indifferent onlookers, and it was that appeal that aroused the anger of the men beating him, and they brought the boards down on him. They didn't seem to be hard blows, because the man in the puddle continued pleading.

"You thought there was no judge and no judgment." They spoke to him with words they remembered from home.

"It wasn't my fault, believe me. There are people who can testify that I helped them."

"The God of vengeance has appeared, the God of vengeance," they howled together and brought the boards down on his back. From there it didn't seem like a real punishment but like a whipping without inordinate cruelty. Nonetheless the man screamed at the top of his lungs.

"Why are they beating him?" the girl asked.

"He was a collaborator," Theo answered curtly.

The sky grew clearer, the hilltops were lit brightly, and people gathered twigs and lit bonfires. The smell of roasted potatoes wafted through the air. Occasionally laughter would slice through the air and be swallowed up.

"Why don't you go and get washed?" he asked the girl, surprisingly.

"You're right." Startled, she stepped away from him.

"Do you have clothes?"

"No." A coarse, womanly laugh spread on her puffy face.

"Everyone managed to get clothes, but only you were too lazy?" He wanted to say that, but he didn't say it.

Meanwhile the men ceased beating their victim and sat down to rest on a rock. The beaten man didn't move out of the puddle. He had collapsed on his knees and sunk in the mud. He looked around him. Fear did not leave his face. His hands constantly scraped the ground as if he were trying to dig himself in.

"Why did you collaborate? Why did you inform?" One of the men who had beaten him addressed him. "You knew you'd be punished sooner or later. Crime doesn't pay."

"What could I do?" he implored them, as though it weren't a matter of life and death but rather some business deal that had gone wrong.

"So, you confess." The man tried to trip him up.

"I didn't collaborate. They forced me. Everyone knows they forced me. I can prove it."

"In a little while the field tribunal is coming here. They'll try you. They know their job."

"I lost everyone. I don't have a relative in the whole world. I alone remain." The man was aroused from his pains.

"Don't say 'I.' " One of the men cut him short.

"How else can I say it?"

"Don't say 'I.' You lost your 'I.' You're a nothing."

Hearing these words the beaten man smiled for some reason. "Can I have something to eat? I haven't eaten since morning."

"You want to eat? You have to fast, to beg forgiveness from people, to crawl and shout out, 'I have sinned.' "

"I'm frightened," said the man. "Don't you see that I'm frightened? You're frightening me," he stammered in a strange flood of words. The men who had beaten him didn't react.

Theo looked up. He found that other people were also standing and looking, in leisurely fashion, more in a spirit of petty malice than in true anger, at the spectacle now taking place. No one reacted or expressed an opinion. It was as though it were not a question of life and death.

"You must wash yourself off. You'll feel better," he told the girl again.

The girl smiled, as if he were talking about some simple action that her mind couldn't grasp. "She's dumb." The thought passed through Theo's mind.

To make certain, she asked, "Where can you wash?"

"Why are you asking? Anywhere. There are plenty of brooks here. Don't you have enough water?"

"Are you sending me away?" She cringed like a rebuked animal.

"I'm not sending you away. You asked, and I answered you. Didn't you ask?"

"I wanted to get washed, of course I wanted to. But I don't have a change of clothes. What's the point of getting washed when you don't have clothes?"

"Your wounds will get full of pus. They're already festering. Didn't you notice?"

Theo sat down. A kind of fatigue, of which he was wary, gradually took hold of him. In vain he tried to overcome it. His eyes closed more and more tightly and he fell asleep.

When he woke up the night was already spread over the hills. Here and there the lights of a bonfire flickered. From the distant declivity people's voices climbed up to where he was with a swelling roar. It was hard to know whether it was a fight or a celebration. In the shallow puddle the beaten man lay in a normal position. His face was smeared with mud but for some reason it didn't look miserable. The beaters had apparently left him to himself and gone away.

"What did you do?" Theo asked him matter-of-factly.

"Nothing. I don't know what they want out of me." He woke up.

"Then why don't you get out of the mud?"

"I'm afraid. The men who beat me warned me that I mustn't dare get out. I'm waiting for the field tribunal. I don't know when it will get here. Maybe you know. I only want a fair trial."

"Do you feel guilty?" Theo raised his voice.

"I lost everyone. I have no one in the world. You certainly understand that."

"You do feel guilty, don't you?"

"How do you know?"

"I can see."

"Could you spare a cigarette? I've suffered more than enough. I've already gotten my punishment in this world. My back's completely broken. They beat me with boards."

Theo handed him a cigarette.

"Thank you kindly. I'll remember you forever. You did a big mitzvah."

"Get out of the mud." Theo spoke to him with disgust.

"I'm afraid. They frighten me more than the Germans. I'll stay here till the end of the proceedings. There's no choice. What can I do? Where can I run? I'm better off here. Maybe some of us will stay alive at any rate."

Theo left him and went back to the hillock. The past few days bore him as though on slow, heavy waves. Now it was as if the waves had stopped flowing. He felt the depression under his feet. "Let's stop a minute. Why hurry?" he said to himself as though he hadn't stopped. A kind of distant fear came and enveloped him. "A person is not an insect," he said to himself. But that very sentence, which he had heard many times with various sorts of expressions, was virtually stuck in his brain. He made a convulsive movement with his head and turned around. The sight was no different here: an evening with the smell of smoke; a few people stood next to campfires and others lay sprawled next to stumps. Two children screamed out loud. It seemed that someone had hit them hard. "Why don't you get up and get out of here?" The words stood ready in his throat. "There are wide-open spaces. Why crowd together in one spot? Haven't we learned that danger lurks in every quarter?" But, as in a dream, his mouth was blocked, his legs were bound, a kind of tremor quivered in his fingers.

"Do you have a cigarette?" A man rose from where he was lying. He was a tall man, dressed in old, faded clothes. His voice showed a kind of old, good delicacy.

"I do," Theo answered and handed him a cigarette.

"I thank you very much," he said, the way they used to say it in Theo's house, with the very same accent.

"You're from Vienna, aren't you?" The words slipped out of Theo's mouth.

"How did you know?" said the man, and a smile of ease spread on his face.

"I noticed your accent."

"I myself have forgotten everything," the man said and lowered his head. "Where do you intend to go?"

"Home, straight home."

"You're right, you're right."

"How am I right?" Theo recoiled.

"In your decision."

It was evident that this delicate face once knew of deliberation and order; now it was as if it had narrowed to a kind of hesitant wonderment. Theo wanted to offer the man some assurance, but the man was so sunk in his loss that he didn't notice Theo's good intention.

"First a person must get home, isn't that so?"

"Correct, my young friend," said the man with great submission.

Now Theo regretted having planted vain hopes in the man's heart. The man felt, apparently, Theo's helplessness, and he said, "It should be obvious, I'm not expecting miracles."

IV

AFTER THAT the days were cold and clear. On the faces of the abandoned hills, in the shadow of low bushes, the refugees lay and did nothing. The informers who had been beaten didn't run away. They lay under a bush. If it weren't for their scratched faces, they wouldn't have been any different from the rest. They too gathered twigs, lit campfires, and drank coffee. The oldest of them never ceased complaining about the cruelty of those who had beaten him. He spoke in a grating, old voice, as though he were only talking about some business deal. But when the man took off his torn shirt and showed his back to his friend, it was evident that his complaint was not idle. The breadth of his back was swollen, strewn with wounds and scars.

"We have to put iodine on your back," said his friend with a tone conveying more than a little repugnance.

"Where can I get iodine?"

"I saw that one of the refugees had a full bottle. You have to look for him."

"I don't care about a thing," the beaten man said, returning the torn shirt to his body and immediately pouring himself a cup of coffee. "One thing I do have to say to you: they were crueler than the Germans."

"They hit me on the feet. They beat me with a rubber hose," his friend answered him, the one who was sitting on the ground with his legs spread out. "Now I can't get away from here. Who knows what they did to my feet. Now, when everyone has been liberated, I'm tied up like a dog."

"You have to rest." His friend acquitted himself with those words.

"True, you're right. Here will be the end of me. I hadn't pictured to myself that it would be right here. Oh well. Everyone has his own end."

"Don't worry. People won't leave you behind." The other one was sparing with his words.

"I'm not worried. I know they'll leave me behind. I wasn't any better than they are. I also left and went on ahead. What do I have to expect from others? Why would other people be better than me?"

"You have to rest and overcome the pain."

"Rest doesn't cure lacerated feet. They ripped my feet to shreds. I'm afraid to undo the rags. Who knows what I'll find there."

"You have to take off the rags to let the wounds breathe. I'm ventilating mine too."

Theo sat at some distance from them and took in every word. Their voices sounded clear and cutting, piercing to the bone.

"You must take off the rags to ventilate the wounds," the man said again in a dry voice, with a kind of frightening practicality.

"I have no desire to see the wounds."

"If you're going to be stubborn, I have nothing to add."

They sat and drank coffee without exchanging another word. It was clear that in a little while they would all move on, but the one with the bandaged feet wouldn't move. No one would come to his aid, not even his companion, who a few minutes before had consoled him with a few superficial words.

Theo wanted to get up and approach them, but they were too sunk into themselves. It was as though they had just grasped that for them the war wasn't over, for them it was continuing. He felt a kind of closeness with them.

Not far from the informers four men sat and played cards. Their bony hands moved with great dexterity. In fact they were trying to hypnotize each other, each one pretending he had the right cards in his hand, the trumps. Emaciation gave strength to their expressions. They had forgotten that just two weeks ago they had been imprisoned, starving for bread, loading coal with wounded hands. Their game bound them like a snare.

Theo walked slowly without going far off. The vigor that had throbbed within him only a few days earlier was drained out of him. He knew: if he only laid his body on the ground, he would be one of them. He forbade himself to lie down and dragged his legs from place to place. Finally, helpless, he collapsed next to a tent.

"Where are you from?" a man asked in a voice from former days, an annoyingly Jewish voice.

"Why do you need to know?" Theo answered with restraint.

"Is it forbidden to ask? You're Jewish like me, it seems."

"It's forbidden to annoy people."

"An innocent question."

"There's no innocence here."

"So what is there here, malice?" the man said, raising his upper body.

"What there is here is thoughtlessness, to be precise."

"I understand you. Now I understand you," said the man, lying back down on the ground.

The evening came with a strong light, and people lit new campfires, roasted potatoes, and argued loudly. Their voices buzzed harshly in Theo's ears. For a moment he wanted to get up and shout: "Silence. No more talking, no more arguments. We need utter silence. It's disgraceful to talk with such loud voices."

Night fell and Theo's fury faded. The people near the fires now seemed short and expressionless, robots walking with strange twitches. "Tomorrow I'm getting away from here. You won't ever see me again." The words quivered in his mouth but weren't audible.

Later he approached one of the fires and asked for a cup of coffee. A woman offered him a cup of coffee earnestly, with trembling hands, immediately adding, "If you want more, we have some. We have plenty."

"This is more than enough for me," Theo said, sitting down where he was.

The coffee was hot and fragrant, and he drank it with thirsty gulps. All the events since his liberation now seemed to him wrapped in thick fog, and here they seemed to be sinking into a sticky dough. "Mina," he suddenly rose and called out loud. No one responded to his cry. He held the cup and gripped it, as though doing his duty.

Before long he fell asleep. The thick fog also coated his sleep. Though he heard, saw, and argued, none of that could extricate him from the dough, and he sank into it.

He saw Mina in his sleep, sitting at some distance from him, but out of reach. A narrow but deep river separated them. "Too bad I didn't sign up for the swimming course," he said. "My mother wouldn't let me because the swimming teacher taught the boys in the Danube rather than in a pool. I'm sorry I listened to her." Mina heard his voice and responded immediately. "The Danube is very dangerous. My parents wouldn't let me swim in it either." "Now I'm disfigured," Theo said, pointing to the informers. Mina examined the informers but didn't find anything wrong with them. "If you saw his back, you'd understand what I'm talking about." "Too bad," said Mina, "that they have no iodine."

"You're concerned about him? About the informer?" Theo was outraged in his sleep. "You left me and went away."

"I didn't leave you. I'm here. In a minute's swim you can get to me."

"Because I didn't learn how to swim, that's why you're going away and leaving me?"

When he awoke the image was still before his eyes. The darkness of the day was mingled with the darkness of night. Apparently the fires had burned all night long, and the people hadn't slept. The woman kept serving coffee with trembling hands. Theo approached her cautiously and asked for a cup of coffee.

"You came just in time," she greeted him. "There's a new pot of coffee."

"Thanks," said Theo, grateful.

"Think nothing of it. Too bad we have no bread. We're out of bread. Take a dry biscuit. They're tasty."

Theo bent his head, stepped back cautiously, and said, "Thank you."

"They're not mine. We found them in the storerooms. The people are thirsty. All during the war they didn't drink. They didn't even give them water. Drink, dearie, this coffee revives the soul."

"Thank you. I have nothing to give you."

"No need. I'm glad to be serving it. If there is some meaning to life, it's coffee. We've lost everything. What do we have left, can you tell me? In any case I can't sleep. From now on, forevermore, I won't sleep. I'm pleased to be serving coffee."

"Are you religious?"

"No, dearie," she said, surprised. "My parents were religious people, but not I. Neither I nor my late husband, nor our children. We didn't go to synagogue. Now I'm sorry we didn't go to the synagogue on holidays. My late husband was a Communist and opposed it vehemently. Why do you ask?"

"It just seemed to me you were a religious woman."

"What can a person do in a place like this? One's thoughts just drive one mad. Do you find anything wrong with what I'm doing?"

"No. I decided to go to a monastery." Theo blurted out the words as though unwillingly. "In a monastery there is space. The people aren't piled up on top of each other. There are walls."

"I," said the woman, "am Jewish. My children were Jewish. I don't know what to say to you."

"I think constantly about a monastery."

"What do you expect to find there?"

"A great deal of quiet and a lot of music. It's hard for me to bear this noise."

"I'm a simple woman, and nothing disturbs me."

"Don't you suffer from the noise?"

"No."

The woman was about fifty years old. Her hands were thin and bony. She had worked loading coal on the docks and so was saved. Her husband and her sons weren't saved. Theo was laden with words and wanted to talk at length about his urgent need to get to monasteries, where there was much quiet, and only there among the high trees was it possible to recuperate. But, as usual at moments of great emotional excitement, the words went mute within him, and he stood frozen and looked at that woman who was standing in the dawn light and, like a maidservant, serving coffee to weary strangers, who did not bother to thank her with even a single word.

When he returned to his place he once again remembered Mina's lovely face. Now it was clear to him that she, like him, had also decided to abandon this life and to enter a convent, and it made no more sense to look for her among the people lying there. He must go out and look for her on other mountains, empty of all people, where the monasteries stood.

Meanwhile one of the refugees began annoying the woman who was serving the coffee and angrily claimed that she was discriminating against him and not giving him bread. The woman swore in all innocence that if she had bread she would gladly give some to him, but she had none, not a single slice.

The man, for some reason, wouldn't leave her alone. He

stood there and pestered her. He was a short, thin refugee who could have been driven away with a sweep of one's hand, but no one mixed in, and he stood where he was and pestered the woman. Theo sat and observed him. At first the man's grimaces didn't anger him, but as he stood there hectoring the woman, Theo finally couldn't bear it. He went over to the man and quietly said to him, "Why are you pestering her?"

"She won't give me bread. She gives to everyone except me."

"This woman doesn't owe you a thing," Theo said curtly.

"Why is she giving bread to everyone, but she won't give any to me?"

"Because she doesn't like you."

The man apparently took note of Theo's fury and withdrew.

From then on Theo sat and watched, and the longer he sat, the angrier he grew. "I could have been far away from here. If it weren't for this delay, I would already have crossed the mountains." The nights didn't bring solace to his soul. On the contrary, the darkness afflicted him with gloom.

While he was sitting there a refugee approached him and said: "Why don't you take something to eat? Down below there's a pile of cans, biscuits, and dried fruit."

"I don't feel like it. I'm not hungry." Theo cautiously rejected the man's suggestion.

"A person must eat." He spoke in an annoying, effeminate voice.

"I'm not hungry." Theo rejected the man's repeated request with restraint.

"You must eat." He wouldn't leave him alone.

"I'm not accountable to anyone. Now I'm a free man. The

labor camps have been liquidated. No one will tell me what
to do." He no longer held himself back.

"I don't want to interfere, perish the thought. But after the
war you've got to regain your strength. Three years of starva-
tion have worn us down, don't you think?"

"What do you want from me?" Theo was going to leave
him.

"Nothing. I'm asking you to eat. Now we have something
to eat. You have to eat to get strong." The man repeated
himself obsessively. Theo knew that the man meant no ill,
and he didn't want to harm him, but still he lost patience and
said, "Don't bother me."

"I mustn't let you perish. I, at any rate, can't permit you."

"Don't talk to me!" Theo raised his voice.

"I won't say another thing," said the man, raising his two
arms and turning to go.

Theo, for some reason, added, "No one should mix into
anyone else's business. For many years we were together. Now
the time has come for everyone to be by himself. That togetherness brought many calamities down upon us. Now it's every
man for himself. Let no one mix into anyone else's business."

"What can I do?" said the refugee. "I can't rid myself of my
former habits. What can I do?"

Theo apparently didn't catch the answer. He kept on saying: "The time has come to separate. Let everyone find whatever resting place he can."

"You're right. I'm a fool. What can I do? It's hard to uproot
old vices." The man walked away. Before long Theo also rose
to his feet. Saying nothing to anyone, he set out on his way.

First he intended to go back to the cabin, but he immediately changed his mind and turned toward the course

which he had stridden for a few days. He left the hills behind with no regret and at a quick pace he slipped into the valley. It was a deep, narrow valley. A sharp fragrance of mown clover stood in the air. Apparently the wind came from a distance. Here, there was not a living soul. Green darkness lay beneath the tree trunks, and the silence was heavy and undisturbed. "I'm on my way," he said to himself. In fact he was glad to be walking away from the refugees. He devoured the road swiftly, without thinking. Before an hour had passed he no longer heard human voices, not even a scrap.

V

An hour's walk distanced Theo from the refugees. Again he was by himself. He sat next to some tree stumps that had sprouted green shoots. The sky was blue and unspotted. The feeling that had driven him at the beginning of his journey returned to him and grew stronger. He was sure that if he advanced along the course he had plotted for himself, in two months he would reach home. That feeling erased the miserable faces of the refugees from his memory. They had stirred up and muddied his soul.

He went out to gather wood immediately. That action, which he performed almost without thinking, made him happy. Before long a pile of twigs was lying in front of the stumps. He lit a match and fire seized the twigs. Pleasant heat surrounded him, and immediately, marvelously, he saw before him the imperial garden, with his mother at his side. From the imperial garden he and his mother had first gone off, secretly, to nearby Hofheim, where two marvels dwelled together: a small lake in whose green waters the thin trees were reflected, and, nearby, an old chapel made of basalt, in the walls of which were carved several lovely statues.

Once a month they would ride or, better, flee there. It was a kind of secret pilgrimage, which was cast in his vision, the vision of a child, with the smells of pine trees sweetly perfuming his sleep. In the imperial garden he saw his mother's hands for the first time, two long, flying hands, that grabbed him and swung him up with joy. "I have a beautiful place, the most beautiful, let's disappear. Let's disappear." That was the magic charm whose power let them float away and disappear for hours. Usually they would reach Hofheim by horse and carriage, and immediately they would go out to the lake. But sometimes his mother would take the tram. The tram used to bring them close to Hofheim, and from there they would climb up to the chapel.

In time he knew that that hidden contact caused his mother great excitement. When she left the chapel tears of joy flooded her face. On those first trips, when he was six, a secret bond was woven between him and his mother. He had no words, but the closeness in those hasty journeys was great. By that time she had already embroidered all her plans for him, and they were rather grandiose plans. Then, of course, he hadn't understood any of her many words. He loved to watch her face. She was beautiful.

After the visit to the chapel they would linger for a while in the inn, The Black Horse. His mother would sip a snifter of cognac, and he would get a tankard of homemade grape juice. If there were coaches in the vicinity, they would return by horse and carriage, but usually they would go back to the tram through the abandoned orchard and go home that way.

"Where did you disappear to?" His father's anxiety would greet them at the door.

"We were in the woods. It was marvelous."

"And has the boy done his lessons?"

The father's entreaties were to no avail. "The boy must study. You're taking him away from school. Because of you he won't be promoted." These arguments had no significance for her. She was obstinate: "If not now, then when?" The next day she would wrap herself up in two blankets and sleep around the clock.

In the first grade he hardly studied at all. He suffered from chest colds and ear infections. On warm days his mother would whisk him right onto the tram and from there to the villages, the churches and chapels. No less exciting were the returns home. Wrapped up next to his mother he loved to look at the tired faces of the workers returning after a day of toil, but even more he loved to observe his mother. In the tram her beauty was splendid.

They visited many villages that year, but little Hofheim remained engraved in his memory with a kind of transparent clarity, because there he had seen his mother as he had never seen her before.

In the second grade he liked to draw, hear music, and sit for hours without doing anything. But more than anything he loved the trips with his mother, mad trips that would last all day. Museums, theaters, churches, and chapels, views of the snow and views of the sunset. More than once he had opened his eyes and found himself in a remote country inn, far from any road, drowsing in his mother's arms.

His father, an inward-looking man who loved order, tried to dissuade his mother from taking these impulsive trips, but nothing could stop her. Usually she would erupt in the morning, after coffee. The look of her eyes would change, and after that neither rain nor snow could stop her. His father could do nothing but say a single word: "Madness."

Sometimes it seemed that she was drawn to bridges. A suspension bridge would thrill her to tears. She would stand by the railing and weep, as if a lost chapter of her life had been revealed in the sight. But sometimes she was drawn to chapels, sinking into them with excited contemplation.

During those half-awakened years they traversed distant and hidden parts, villages, medicinal springs, and castles known to but a few. He would be absent from school for whole days, but that was the charm. While everybody else was toiling over their homework, he was coasting along rivers, swallowing up the distances in elegant trains. Of course his father boiled, but what could he do? He hadn't the power to hold back that eruption. He would sink his bitterness into the bookstore he tended with such care. From time to time, nevertheless, he would try to stand his ground. "The boy hasn't gone to school for a week. He won't be promoted. You're driving him out of his senses."

"He's not missing a thing," she would answer with shocking calm.

"His grades aren't so brilliant. You know, they're quite bad."

"No matter. He'll catch up. There's time."

"I raise my hands and stop my mouth." With those words his father would admit defeat.

Afterward his mother would be absent from home for weeks. Maids would come and go. Now his father was with him for hours; they would read stories and do homework together. This was a different father, calm. He would serve breakfast by himself, with measured movements. At seven they would go out together, his father to his store and Theo to school. In the evening they would sit and listen to music.

All that dry pleasure would stop at once when his mother returned. She would appear, without warning, like a storm. His father knew that she was liable to surprise them, but he still would freeze in place whenever she did appear.

That year he heard the cold word "sanatorium" for the first time. He heard it from the maid, and it was immediately engraved in his memory.

"Mother is living in a sanatorium now, isn't that so?"

"How do you know?" His father was fearful.

"Cecilia told me."

"Soon she'll come back," his father said curtly.

Like a storm she would return home, and the household routines would change immediately. No more school, homework, or books, but trips in boats and trams. In vain his father would try to halt her momentum. "Give me a raincoat," she would order. "I'm going out."

First it seemed she had plans, but quickly everything would go awry, they would get stuck in out-of-the-way places, in neglected country hotels, waiting in railroad stations for hours, eating stale sandwiches and finally falling asleep on a bench in a public park.

The trips would mostly end as they had begun, with no visible cause. Weariness or mortification would bring them back home. Once she told the owner of a restaurant, "If this is the food you have to offer us, we're going home," and indeed, they returned on the first train.

Afterward she would sit in the living room, wrapped in blankets, looking at magazines or listening to music. The maids would change every month, because they refused to obey her instructions. With her everything went according to her moods, sometimes up, sometimes down. Frequently she would talk softly to the maid as to a younger sister.

When there was no maid in the house, pots and plates would pile up in the kitchen sink, disorder would invade as far as the living room. That was one of the excuses for her trips. "It's hard for me to bear this house. It makes me sad. Let's get out of here. The time has come for someone to serve me a cup of coffee and a nice slice of cake. No one pays attention to me. I'm going to Café Pat, where they like me and serve strawberries and cream and a cheesecake that deserves to be world-famous. What am I doing here?"

He came to be closely acquainted with that tangle. Once, for no visible reason, she threw off her blankets and stood in the center of the living room, shouting: "Be off, robbers! I should be living in Vienna, not here. The provinces are eating me alive. Everything is dead inside me." After that the stream of words grew stronger. Past and present, people and places, everything was in a seething mixture. Her voice changed and he didn't recognize it. Soon two attendants from the sanatorium came. First they spoke pleasantly to her. When their entreaties proved useless, they dragged her out to the ambulance.

That night his father spoke to him about her illness for the first time, about the moods that overcame her and the need to hospitalize her in the sanatorium. He formed an image of the sanatorium as a house with tall, white rooms, heavy iron keys stuck in the locks, no one entered or left, in the evening a servant would come inside wordlessly and throw a few logs into the stove.

He stayed with his father. On Sundays they would go to the park together. These trips never had the splendor and glory of excursions with his mother. Everything in its time, and in measure. Nothing unusual, no surprises. In the evenings too: no surprises or cries of amazement. The maid would prepare meals and serve them in the pantry, and whatever was placed on one's plate was eaten up completely.

If it weren't for the fear that his mother might surprise them, life would have continued evenly. That fear darkened the house and made it feel smaller at every hour of the day. Once she appeared in the middle of the night, dressed in a fur coat, with the gestures of an actress. There was no sign of anything bad in her face, only a kind of exaltation. She immediately began showering Theo with kisses. Theo was bewildered, and in his great confusion he shouted, "Why did you wake me up?" That brought his gay mother to tears. "Theo doesn't love me either."

Theo did love her, and he wasn't afraid of her, even when she shouted out loud, and with the passing years he seemed to understand her better. On more than one occasion he resolved, "Tomorrow I'm taking the local to visit my mother, no matter what." He learned to love his father later, but never openly. His father was well versed in mathematics and Latin, and Theo sometimes needed his help. Occasionally his father would say, "Too bad Mama isn't at home." That was a kind of stifled groan, showing that his father had once loved her. But his father passed most of the hours of the day in the store. He didn't permit himself to come home for a rest in the afternoon. In the evening fatigue was visible in every one of his movements. In time Theo learned: the household expenses were many, beyond his means.

During one of his vacations his mother told him that after high school she had studied for two years at the Hermann Himmel Art School. Why had her studies been nipped in the bud? She didn't tell him.

For two years she had lived with her parents and done nothing. Afterward she had married Theo's father. She was pretty and proud. Her quirks were taken as the caprices of an only daughter, a pretty girl. Her parents, until their deaths, had never accepted the doctors' opinion that their daughter was ill. They were certain that her husband, his taciturnity and his stinginess, had made her sick.

Theo's father, an intellectual with good manners, could have been a university lecturer, but he preferred the provinces to the city, business to research. Immediately after the wedding he opened the bookstore. In a few months the shop was well known throughout the area.

After Theo's birth his mother was seized by restlessness and fears. She fired one maid, and another, thin and short, was brought in to take her place. But she wasn't satisfied with this one either. She would spend the morning downtown, in clothing and cosmetics shops. In the afternoon she would return with two bundles in her arms, full of happiness. She would spend the rest of the day in front of the mirror. At night fatigue and melancholy would overcome her, and she would wrap herself in a blanket and weep.

"Why are you crying?" his father would whisper. In fact there was no need to ask. The living room told the whole story. In the living room were disorderly piles of winter and summer clothes, which his mother would generously give away to the maids and to poor people. Money meant nothing to her. She squandered it heedlessly. His father's pleas were useless. When he scolded her, she would burst into tears. Immediately the words went silent in his mouth.

He went out very early and came home at night. The few words he was used to saying were lost to him. His life came to be centered on the store, where the girl at the cash register served him cheesecake and a cup of coffee every day at ten. There he would doze off on the sofa between two and three. True, the shop flourished, but the household expenses, two maids, the clothes and cosmetics, grew from week to week. The time came when they had to use their savings, the jewelry. In the end, having no choice, loans. "Why do you waste so much money?" His pleas fell on deaf ears. She squandered, and he had to pay her debts in the town's stores.

In vain Theo's father tried to stop her running around. She was obstinate: "The boy must see treasures. School doesn't show him a thing. If not now, when?" Thus began those trips, giving Theo the strong impression that time was nothing but a train that one changed every two hours.

At that time she was already prone to occasional attacks. Her face would wither all at once, she would sink down in an armchair, wrap herself in a blanket, and complain of the cold. Between attack and attack she would gather her wits, get dressed, and announce: "We're on our way!" The trips would restore softness and beauty to her face. They would sit for hours in lonely inns, looking at the landscape and listening to music.

Later, when he was already in high school, the attacks would also seize her while she was traveling. Once she stood on a bridge and shouted: "I love this water, only this water. I'll drink it to the last drop." Because words were useless, an attendant had to drag her to the doctor to give her an injection of a sedative.

One evening, without taking off his coat, Theo's father announced: "We must separate. I haven't the strength to bear these debts."

"What?" Her mouth gaped.

"I have no more strength." It was evident the words had been prepared in his mouth for a long time. Now he threw off the burden. Hearing the announcement, his mother hugged two thick pillows and said, "I surrender."

At that time hooligans were already gathering in the streets, and control of the city council passed to the Nazis. Anyone with a penny or two escaped. As usual the ones left were the weak, the poor, the indecisive, and those who believed that no ill could befall them.

Theo's father, for some reason, was firmly of the opinion that the separation must be made by those who had presided over the wedding, the rabbis. The old rabbi, abandoned and ill, would invite the couple once every two weeks. Theo would accompany his mother to the rabbi's house. Two other rabbis, even older, took part in the deliberations. Regarding the division of property, his father's position was clear: it all belonged to her. That enabled the three rabbis to formulate the bill of divorce. Still, one of them couldn't restrain himself, and he asked, "Why now?"

His father's answer was prompt: "I can't bear it any longer, rabbi."

"In a time of troubles we must support each other," the old man murmured.

His mother, who was usually flooded with words and gestures, didn't intervene in the deliberations. From the rabbi's house she went right to her armchair and wrapped herself in cushions.

In the final session his mother spoke this sentence: "I don't deserve this." There was a big uproar in the place, and no one paid attention to her. Afterward she never left the house anymore. Wrapped in cushions and blankets she would talk to herself, using the third person, as though it weren't she, but another woman. She never got angry at anyone, not at her parents, and not at her former husband. She had always loved to indulge in baby talk. Now it came back to her, giving her face a strange youthfulness.

Because she never went out, the evil tidings sounded to her like storms that would pass. She spoke often about the coming spring, about a visit to the Tyrol, and maybe they would take a cruise to Italy. Theo used to sit next to her for hours. His father would come once or twice a week, loaded down with whatever he could obtain.

The doctors' opinion was clear. She had to be hospitalized as soon as possible, and forever. Since there was no money, father and son decided to sell the house immediately. Theo's mother spoke of the sale with enthusiasm, as though they were about to exchange a modest home for a castle.

The sale, of course, never took place. The deportations came one after the other, at regular intervals. His mother was deported before them, for some reason. She went to the train dressed carefully, as she used to go to railroad stations in the past. She refused to take a knapsack. As she left the house she looked very lovely. Her illness wasn't visible in her. Expressions of pride and softness were mingled in her face.

VI

As HE WALKED ENERGETICALLY, clinging to his course and sure he was drawing farther away from the refugees, he saw two tents nearby. The tents were carelessly made and seemed abandoned. He could have ignored them and turned to the right. But he immediately discovered that tents were also scattered to the right of the hill, with smoking campfires among them. The smell of coffee hung in the air. "I'll never get away from them." He stopped where he was. The silent afternoon hour lay upon the thin vegetation. A few old knapsacks were leaning against tree trunks, and it was clear no one cared what happened to them.

"Where're you coming from and where're you heading?" An old, familiar-sounding voice surprised him.

"Home," Theo answered.

"It's good that someone knows he has a home. I don't have anything."

"I don't have anything either, but I'm walking. One mustn't be idle." Theo found words to reproach him.

"I've walked up to now, but I got tired. Allow me to offer you a mug of coffee. Fresh coffee."

"Thank you."

"Have a roll. Yesterday there was a woman here who baked these rolls. This morning she went off and left them. At first I too had a lot of energy. Now it's used up."

"We have to advance." Theo spoke with assurance.

"You're right." The man's large body had saved him. Now that giant husk was bent over, as if it had been emptied. A kind of drunken gaze covered his eyes like a scab.

"This is the worst place of all. Isn't that obvious? Why are the people all crowded into one place?"

"It's easier to be together, isn't it?"

"That's an illusion. Or, rather, a delusion." Theo raised his voice.

"You're right. I hadn't thought of that." The man bent his head.

"I decided to get away. I'm not crowding in anymore."

"If I knew where to go, I too would get away."

"You should go home. Isn't that obvious?"

"Where is your home, if I may ask?"

"Baden-bei-Wien."

"Interesting. My parents used to go there in the summer. I was never there. My parents told me a lot about the place. Have a roll."

"Thanks."

"My pleasure. I have more than enough. Anyway, I'll leave most of the supplies behind me. Who can drag sacks of coffee, sugar, and bottles of French cognac?"

"Why did you hoard so much?"

"A good question. Two days ago, when I dragged away the sacks, I was sure I was doing the smartest thing. You're moving along without a thing, I see."

"Correct."

"I envy you. I'm a total fool. It's fear. I'm ashamed. I'm afraid to be left alone. If there's drink, you can offer some to people. They sit with you for an hour or two."

"In the meantime you've helped people." Theo tried to console him.

"I'm no saint, believe me."

While Theo was sipping the coffee, the man made a gesture very familiar to him. At first it seemed like a disparaging gesture, but a second glance told him that it wasn't only the gesture that was familiar to him.

"Uncle Salo," he wanted to cry out, but his voice was stifled in his throat, as in a dream.

Uncle Salo, his father's eldest brother, would appear at the house on rare occasions. But his few appearances made a great impression. A sturdy merchant of the old school, for whom the world was divided into two parts: those who toil and those who, for some reason, refuse to toil. He admired the ones who toiled, while idle people repulsed him. He hated his sister-in-law with a passion. For him she embodied the essence of idleness, sloppiness, and capriciousness, and he concealed that opinion neither from his brother nor from his sister-in-law. Even as he entered the house he would inspire Theo's mother with dread. She would shut herself up in her room and not leave it until he departed. He knew very well what he was doing, but he wouldn't leave. And to make his opinion heard, he would talk loudly, and the effect, of course, was incomparably more terrifying.

It wasn't always that way. There were years when Theo's father would defend his wife steadfastly. But Uncle Salo never gave in. His hostility was persistent and unbroken, as though she wasn't a weak woman but rather a tenacious enemy who mustn't be let alone.

Later on his father no longer found words to defend his wife. Uncle Salo's voice rang loudly through the house. He was suspicious of Theo. He would say: "A creature with a weak character, who should be immunized against weakness and kept at a distance, because of the noxious influence of his mother." Once he said: "Idle people spread melancholy. You have to be careful of them, so they won't upset the mental equilibrium of the industrious." Industrious people were the main pillar of his life. If you met him just once, you could never uproot him from your heart.

And now here he was. The war had changed him, but not completely. That industrious right hand, which had hoarded the supplies, was as if chided by the left hand. He sat on a piece of canvas, with his legs crossed, drinking coffee.

Theo raised his eyes. Uncle Salo was wrapped in another costume. Only scraps remained of his previous incarnation.

"An error," said Theo.

"Who are you looking for?" The man's face showed fully. It wasn't Uncle Salo, but someone who looked like him, the incarnation of an industrious merchant, who supported his household with great toil. His industry had not always stood him in good stead. During the war, wanting too much to be in the forefront, he was the first to be sent to his death.

Theo felt a kind of closeness to the man and said, "Why don't you leave everything behind and get going? Walking is preferable to sitting still. Sitting only brings evil thoughts."

"Correct. You're right. Thoughts are poisoning me."

"What are you thinking about?" Theo tried to be forth-coming.

"About myself. I'm ashamed to admit it. But I have to. I've lost everyone, my wife and my two daughters—and I still think about myself. I hoard sacks. It's stupid. Even worse—evil. You understand me."

"What do you think will happen?" Theo wanted to walk with him a short way.

"That strange preoccupation with oneself is a sin which cannot be atoned for. It disgusts me."

"Are you a religious man?" Theo asked cautiously.

"No, my friend. I come from a middle-class home. Generations of merchants, whom trade, to tell the truth, did not always favor. But one thing it *did* develop in them was a good measure of egotism."

"What do you want to do?"

"What do you mean? To free myself of fear. I was in seven camps. My mother and sisters perished. Still, I'm afraid. Why am I afraid? What am I afraid of?"

Theo looked at him again: a broad, sturdy body. Even his poses were those of a wholesaler, the very image of his Uncle Salo. But the hidden wound plagued him, giving him no rest. Words that were not his own flooded him. He wanted to pull himself free, but he didn't know how. Finally he said, "I should stand on the main road and give out coffee to every passerby, and instead, I surround myself with these commodities. I'm vermin. Why am I vermin? I could have stood erect on the main road and given coffee to every wandering soul. I would have won the right to exist. I would sleep at night. But instead I went and hoarded. Shamelessly. You understand that. Can you please explain it to me?"

For a moment Theo wanted to draw close to the man with a few soft words, but because he could find no words of consolation, he said: "My mother was a spendthrift, and my father never forgave her for it."

"One has to squander." He interrupted Theo. "All my life I hoarded like a stupid beast. Three years in the camp didn't change me. Apparently you can't change people. This selfishness is driving me crazy. Do you understand me?"

Afterward the sky grew clearer. Theo drank a few cups of coffee one after the other, and sat there silently. For a while he was wrapped up in himself and in the taste of the coffee. The man peeled some potatoes in the meantime and put the pot on the fire. Theo watched his movements intently. It seemed to him that the man was in danger, and that he had to be protected. The last words he said had denuded his face of its angry expression. His face was left bare and unprotected. "I won't leave you. I'll be with you and help you. We can open a stand. Don't be afraid," Theo wanted to say, but the man beat him to it and offered him a plate of boiled potatoes. The light in the sky grew broader and broader, and the man's face seemed even barer. Theo moved to the side and curled up next to a short tree. The man's closeness suddenly frightened him.

Before the deportation, Theo remembered, his mother had embroidered a large yellow Star of David on his jacket. She sat in the living room, and for many days she kept busy doing that. Since no one came into the house, he would sit by her side and watch her hands. She would dream out loud about journeys in the spring. Theo didn't mix in. Occasionally he would ask a question, which would only heighten the stream of her visions.

Even in the worst days of her illness she would stand by the window to hear the choir in the church. For years she had followed them. She knew the members of the choir by name. A day without music would bring her to tears. Once she opened the window and called out loud: "Where's the choir? Where's the organist? Without music life has no meaning." Immediately afterward she was seized with trembling and curled up in bed. Before the deportation she was roused to renewed purpose. She went to the train in an exalted mood, dressed in fine clothes, her face clear, unstained.

"Will you have a drink? I have a bottle of French cognac," the man said and his face immediately revived.

They had a few drinks, and, for dessert, some sausage that the man had gotten from a Russian soldier. All the elevated subjects that had concerned him before seemed to be forgotten. He spoke about cognac and everything contained in it. He told two jokes that had once circulated in the camps. In a short while his happiness evaporated. His face went naked again, and that same transparent, blue expression returned and covered it. "It's good you're going home," said the man. "I'm afraid to go back. I don't know what's in store for me there. I see a white wall all the time." The man spoke to himself, but it seemed to Theo, for some reason, that the man doubted his intention of cutting himself off from the refugees and returning home as soon as possible.

"I'm returning home, and without delays this time." The words emerged from Theo's mouth.

"I believe you," said the man.

"It seems to me that you doubt my intention."

"I'm only wondering what you'll do there alone." The man spoke in an old, fatherly voice.

"I'm going to convert."

"To Christianity?"

"Indeed."

Theo hadn't been going to express that intention to him. In fact, until he spoke the words out loud, he hadn't known about it. But, having said it, he wouldn't retract it.

"Strange," said the man, turning pale. "What brought you to that difficult decision?"

"Faith." Theo purposely spoke abruptly.

The man poured himself a full glass and drank it down in a gulp. Evidently that single word spoken by Theo had stunned him. He put the glass down on the ground, lit a cigarette, and didn't remove it from his mouth. Later, as though distractedly, he said, "What harm did the Jews ever do you?"

"It's hard for me to bear that togetherness."

"You can go far away, if that's what you want."

"I did that very thing, but I always found myself with the refugees again. A few days ago I left a camp with the clear intention of getting far away, and look, I found myself here again. It's a closed circle, hard to break out of."

"I wouldn't convert under any circumstances," the man said, with a thin chuckle that whined in Theo's ears like a saw. "I despise graven images. Graven images have always inspired me with disgust. A housemaid lived in our house, very devout in her faith, and it always made me angry to see her down on her knees. It's contempt for humanity, don't you understand?"

"I'm used to it. My mother took me to churches to hear the music."

"I see," said the man, and it was evident that Theo's words made him choke with indignation. Nonetheless he managed to pronounce the following sentence: "Aren't I allowed to despise graven images without being accused of prejudice?"

Theo was surprised by that way of putting it, but he did not concur. "I," said Theo, "I have only pleasant memories of the church. My mother used to take me to church just about every week. No Bach festival would pass without my mother taking me to it. Music preserved my sanity in the darkest of times."

"Now you want to be there all day long?"

"Not all day long. Just every time they play Bach."

"I see," said the man, and it was clear he had no words to express his anger. In the end he found something to say: "One can listen to Bach without converting. It's hard for me to see a person throwing himself down on his knees, confessing and kissing the priest's hand."

"When one does it out of faith, nothing about it is strange."

"How, sir, did you come to that?" the man said, suddenly switching to a more formal mode of address. He poured himself another glass of brandy. "It interests me to know how a Jew came to have faith in Jesus. You must tell me, sir. It's beyond my understanding. I raise my hands in surrender."

"How can words explain to you?" Theo answered in the same formal tone. "But if you insist on asking, sir, I shall explain: Bach's cantatas saved me from death. That was my nourishment for two and a half years."

"Doesn't that frighten you?" The man switched back to a familiar tone.

"Why? I'm going back to the church because Bach dwells there."

"Your intention gives me the chills." The man couldn't restrain himself any longer.

"What did I do wrong?"

"It frightens me more than the gallows square of the camp. Now do you understand?"

"I'm doing it willingly, without fear."

"To my mind it's far worse than any death."

"If a person believes that Jesus bore our sicknesses and torments and will redeem us, should he be shunned for that?"

"I don't understand a single word you just said. I don't want to understand. Do whatever you wish, but please leave me alone. Your presence drives me out of my senses."

Theo wanted to say a few sentences, which were ready in his mouth, but seeing the anger in the man's face, he ceased. "You are very angry at me," he said anyway.

"It isn't anger," said the man. "It's strangulation."

"I don't know what to say to you. You don't want me to lie to you."

"I'm not religious," said the man in a low voice. "But your intention inspires me with a kind of fear that I can't control. It's hard for me to explain. I don't have the words to explain it to you. You can sit here as much as you please, but as for me, with your permission, I'm leaving." Theo heard all the words the man said to him with a kind of sharp clarity, even the phrase "with your permission," which the man had marked with a kind of extra emphasis.

"I'll go. This is your spot," said Theo as he stood up.

"I'd rather get going and leave you everything than sit here. Even if you go away, it would be hard for me to sit here."

"I would have liked to hear you." Theo used a distant expression.

"Why are you tormenting me?"

"I don't mean to torment you."

"The thought that someone who was in a camp until just a

month ago should set out for his native city in order to convert to Christianity drives me mad. That's all. I have nothing to add. I have no intention of adding anything. You understand?"

"I understand," Theo said curtly.

"If you understand, why don't you leave me alone?" the man said, coming up to Theo and grabbing his coat. That movement was strong and threatening, but for some reason it didn't frighten Theo. He froze where he was and didn't utter a word. His restraint apparently aroused the man's anger, and he grabbed his coat again. Theo shook his right hand free, and with a motion that was not intended to be forceful, he pushed the man away. The push was apparently too strong. The man tumbled over a few times and lay still.

The place suddenly fell silent. From the nearby hilltop a woman's voice was heard, a moderate, practical voice, one that seemed to ignore everything that was happening here. Theo felt his knees go weak, and he sank down on them. That movement sharpened his sight, and he immediately noticed that a spurt of blood was rolling down the man's forehead. "What's the matter with you?" he called, as though he hadn't done the deed. The man didn't respond. Theo could see that the man was wounded. His face was drawn, and his lower body was tensed. "What's the matter with you?" Theo called again, loudly.

He hadn't meant to sound a warning, but some people heard his cry and came over. It was clear to everyone just who had done the hitting and who had been hit. A woman knelt next to the fallen man and placed a cloth on his face. The cloth absorbed the blood and turned red. In vain the people tried to get a word out of him. "He's breathing," the woman announced, but other than that there was no sign of life. They didn't pay attention to Theo, as though he hadn't hit the man, but had happened upon the place by accident. The comforting words the people showered down on the fallen man showed affection mingled with dread. They apparently knew him very well.

Later, when all efforts had failed, the woman wrung her hands and said, "I begged him not to go away. Why be alone? All kinds of troubles plague you when you're alone." Theo felt pressure in his chest. The pressure spread through his legs and settled in his feet.

Before long one of the older men turned to Theo and spoke loudly: "What happened here?" Theo hastily explained.

"It looks as if you pushed him too hard." The man summed it up for himself and went back to his place. The others didn't move. The woman wrung out the cloth and put it back on the stricken man's face. She immediately began spouting words. She drew out her words and spoke comfortingly about the need to be together. The people around her absorbed her arguments but didn't respond. Meanwhile, the old man returned with several mugs of coffee. There was moderation in his movements, and goodwill, as though he had grasped that this was the most useful action for the moment. He also handed Theo a mug. Theo grasped the mug with both hands.

"What happened? I don't understand," someone asked distractedly.

"I pushed him, not on purpose," answered Theo.

"Why did you push him?"

"He was holding my coat, and I wanted to free myself."

"You surely said something to him."

"I told him I wanted to convert to Christianity."

"Were you serious?"

"Yes, I was."

"Now I understand," said the man. "I would have shaken you as well."

"The doctor, the doctor. Bring the doctor." The woman suddenly raised her voice and immediately took the cloth off the stricken man's forehead.

"Who'll pay?"

The answer wasn't long in coming. "There's money," said the woman.

Both the question and the answer were in German, the Viennese German Theo knew so well. It was clear to him that his trial had already begun. Soon the doctor would come and determine the degree of damage. He could get up and run away. But he was already bound to his spot, as if in a nightmare.

Meanwhile the woman came back and spoke of the need to be together. There was no beauty in her voice, just an unpleasant monotone that evoked the image of a small, dark grocery store, damp and mildewy.

The doctor arrived accompanied by a young man who carried his bag of instruments. He didn't have to be shown the way. The patient lay on the ground right in front of him.

"When did this happen?"

"Half an hour ago," said the woman, panting.

"What's his name?"

"Paul."

"And what's his family name?"

"We don't know."

The doctor pulled off the stricken man's shirt. Everyone sat tensely and observed the examination.

"What happened?" asked the woman.

"He mustn't be moved. In a little while I'll come back. I have an urgent case down below. A young man tried to commit suicide."

"And what shall we do in the meantime?"

"Nothing."

The people seemed riveted to their places. A sentence had been passed, clearer and sharper than the doctor's voice.

"Why did I let him go?" said the woman, in motherly tones.

"You talked with him a lot, but he didn't want to listen to you. He was drinking too much recently."

"True. Why didn't I have the courage to prevent him?"

"You're not his mother." The man spoke as briefly as he could.

That short sentence, tossed away, silenced the people in an instant.

"I'm six years older than he, and I may regard myself as his older sister," the woman insisted.

"He didn't want to listen to you."

"That's my fault. I didn't know how to talk to him."

"You're exaggerating."

The doctor didn't return. Once again someone called out loudly: "Doctor, doctor, where's the doctor?" Down below next to one of the tents, crouching on his knees, the doctor was treating the suicide. He had apparently cut his veins savagely.

"Why did you do it?" The man approached Theo.

"I didn't mean to," Theo said, rising to his feet.

"Look what you've done."

"I don't know what to tell you." Theo mustered his strength.

"You should be dealt with like the informers." The man spoke briefly and turned away.

Theo didn't sit down again. He followed the people's movements tensely. Among the nearby tents people sat by campfires, drank coffee, and chatted. The relaxed voices reminded him of a resort where he and his mother had spent a summer. That distant memory made him forget his plight. "If the people all about you are tranquil, the sentence won't be very severe." The thought passed through his mind.

Before long reality came and slapped him in the face again. The woman who just a moment before had expressed maternal pity drew close to him and, with a contemptuous movement, said, "Get out of here. I don't want to see you again."

"I'm prepared to stand trial," said Theo. "If I deserve punishment, I'll bear it."

"What kind of trial are you talking about? You killed him."

"I?"

"You."

As the woman spoke, the stricken man opened his eyes: frozen, expressionless eyes. Since no one had expected to see his eyes again, it seemed like a strange sign from heaven. The people knelt down in their places, not believing what they saw.

VII

THEO SET OUT that very night without delay. The trail turned out to be wide open and paved with gravel.

After an hour of walking, he felt a stab of pain in his right shoulder. The pain spread to his neck, climbed up the left side of his face, and stuck there. "It's a passing pain," he remembered his mother saying. She would sometimes call her headaches bad attacks that one had to ignore. During the last year she used to say, "Molten metal in my head."

He sat down where he was. The empty plain frightened him. He looked for cover, but in the whole darkened plain there wasn't even a stump to lean on. Chunks of darkness, like giant tangled knots, slowly drifted toward the few openings remaining on the horizon. Before long those openings were stopped. Thick darkness filled the plain to its brim. Theo closed his eyes, and the sight of the man he had pushed rose before his eyes, leaning on his right arm, the trickle of blood welling up on his forehead, flowing down to the crease of his neck as though to a small lake; the woman kneeling by his side, who could have been either a Jewish woman or a peasant, firmly committed to saving his life. The people around were like plainclothes police.

"What did you do to him, you murderer?"

"He was gripping me. If he hadn't grabbed me, I wouldn't have pushed him. I pushed him lightly." Theo raised his voice.

"What did that man do to you? What could he have done to you? Why did you push him with such cruelty?" The question was cold and cut into his flesh. Theo was about to answer, but the words were throttled in his throat. He knew that any answer of his would only increase the man's anger.

"You'll sit here till the tribunal comes and judges you. They'll decide whether you pushed him softly or hard. Only they can determine how hard it was," the man said, turning aside.

"I should never have deviated from my path." Theo ignored the man's anger. "If I had gone straight, this disaster wouldn't have happened to me. One must remain faithful to his path." That old cliché burst from his lips. And indeed he rose to his feet and set out. Fear seeped into his entire body. He felt heavy, and his legs were hobbled. It was clear to him that the men were organizing in their tents, and the next day they would surround him on all sides. That passing thought hurried his steps. Before long he tripped and fell.

He was still trying to get to his feet when he saw the front door open and there was his father standing in the doorway, wearing a brown suit. For a moment he stood on the threshold, wondering whether he had come to the right place. That is how he used to return home in the evening.

"Max," sometimes his wife used to address him from where she was sitting in the armchair, the way one talks to a servant at home who hasn't shut the door.

"What?" His father's reply was not slow in coming.

"What time is it?"

"Eight."

"It's still early. Why am I cold? Why haven't they lit the stoves in the house? A house without a stove is like a cellar."

His father's presence in the house wasn't real. His mother filled the house, with no space left over. Even on Sundays, when he used to sit at the table in the living room and drink coffee, his existence lacked reality. Since he spoke little, his voice always sounded loud and strange. There was a kind of strident opposition between his height and the breadth of his shoulders and his lack of presence. That was very noticeable at night. It always seemed as if he had already left. His mother, from the dawn of his memories, was talkative, laughing, churning up a spirit of confusion and dragging him from place to place. That's how her voice would sound: "Forget about everything, dearest, and let's go out into the wide world. This house is driving me crazy. People who sit at home are narrow-minded, but we won't let that narrowness take possession of us. We have, thank God, aspirations and yearnings for higher things." Those haughty words, which his mother would sometimes speak with assurance, would cast a kind of sadness over his father. His erect posture would collapse all at once.

His father was always at a loss for words. The few words that he spoke were rough, out of proportion, and apparently irrelevant. "I don't understand what you're talking about," his mother would sometimes remark to him. His mother, who used to take her wishes for facts, would address her husband and demand clarity from him. She sometimes caught him in a contradiction, which would befuddle him absolutely. "You're right," he would blurt out with the submission of a scolded child.

When he was angry the words stuck in his mouth even more, and sounded like a muffled rumble. But mostly he would stand silent. He hadn't the strength to withstand the torrent of his wife's words. Sometimes a few sentences would escape his mouth, all at once showing the clumsiness of his large body, and then for a moment it would seem that he was going to lift up the heavy living room table and turn it upside down. In time, when his wife's illness became graver, he stopped talking. His comings and goings were hardly noticeable. "Papa," Theo would sometimes address him. "What?" He would be surprised and withdraw to his room. In the final year of high school Theo happened to go into the bookstore, and he saw a surprising sight: his father was standing at the counter in conversation with a student. He spoke in long sentences with elegant relative pronouns and a few fine adjectives. His stance was calm and simple, with no awkwardness. For a moment Theo wanted to approach him, but his father was deep in conversation, and Theo went out without saying a word. In his junior year of high school they would sit on the balcony and solve algebra problems together. Sitting together did not bring them closer to each other. They never spoke about his mother's illness, as though they had an agreement not to touch upon that secret. "Papa is a busy man. Books interest him more than people." His mother surprised him.

There was no bitterness in her voice. It was as if she were pointing out a well-known fact.

His mother's illness had cast a spell on his childhood and youth, a spell that spread out over years and grew deeper with time. As with all spells, there was expectation, fear, and relief. In vain his father tried to stop her. As long as her soul was in her, she sailed off. One place led to another, one inn pursued another. There was no restraining her lust for that pleasure. The disappointments, of course, were not long in coming, and they were as poignant as her joy. More than once she would stand in a bustling railroad station and cry like a little girl whose parents had abandoned her. "Mama," he would plead, but to no avail. But afterward as well, when she was housebound, her words were marvelously colorful. He would sit by her side for hours and listen to music. Sometimes he would ask her something. She would immediately invoke waves of throbbing words from within herself.

He didn't realize the depth of her illness until the end of high school, and even then not in its full severity. In truth he didn't want to know. Occasionally she would surprise him with a clear perception. "My mother never placed great hopes in my talents, and she was right. I'm incorrigibly sentimental." She spoke very little about her own parents. They died one after the other while still young. Once she said, "I'm like my mother. She too was a wounded bird. Without wings one can't take off, isn't that so? Still we try and try." She chuckled. "I won't give up the effort. I'll always keep trying to take off." Indeed she did not give up.

The father knew that his son was also not under his control. His mother enthralled him with her charms. On more than one occasion his father tried to speak with Theo, but the words he spoke were so thin and so jumbled that they gave the impression of being perfunctory.

In the last year his father grew a little closer to him. It was a brief closeness that came too late. The divorce was in the works, and the biweekly meetings were held from three to five. All three of them would go together. The walk along shady and quiet Schoenbau Street gave that hour a strange kind of festivity. Sometimes his mother would recount some funny episode, make gay remarks, as though they weren't separating but rather about to drink a cup of coffee in a place delightful to the eye.

Afterward too in the miserable room, laden with the odors of lysol and tobacco, the smile never left her lips. They would sit together on the round and fraying sofa. Sometimes the discussion didn't sound like a family quarrel but rather negotiations over abstract matters, and for a moment it seemed to him that his father and mother weren't divorcing, but that he was being divorced from his father. But hardest of all were the rabbis' impassioned pleas to the couple: "This isn't the time for divorce. War is looming on the threshold."

His mother responded with smiles. She called her husband by affectionate names, and every time they mentioned her maiden name she would blush. She apparently hadn't grasped the substance of the matter. Then for the first time he heard his father say hard, full sentences: "Free me of these bonds. I cannot bear it any longer. I am losing my mind."

Angry, his mother didn't respond. She stood her own ground: summer journeys. She spoke of them with a kind of great enthusiasm, without forgetting the details, like the suitcases. At first they would let her speak freely, and indeed she didn't hesitate. But as the deliberations continued, they would interrupt her and silence her. Then, on the same fraying sofa, hostility for his father cropped up, hidden but strong hostility. For many days Theo hated his father, in fact he never forgave him.

His father was progressively erased from his memory and forgotten. In the camp his mother's beauty overwhelmed him. He clung to the thought that immediately after the war, with no delays, he would head for Baden-bei-Wien to meet his mother. He was certain he would find her sitting on the armchair in the living room, wrapped in blankets as always.

Suddenly, without warning, his father left his prison and stood before him, dressed in his regular suit, the brown one, a tall, broad-shouldered man, with embarrassed eyes in contrast with his sturdy build. At first glance Theo didn't recognize him, but when he took off his coat and hung it on the hanger, Theo knew: he had returned from the store and in a little while he would enter the kitchen to prepare his meager meal.

"Papa." The word left his mouth. His father, surprised that anyone still remembered him, didn't linger but immediately entered the kitchen to prepare dinner for himself. Mother never made him dinner. She sat in the living room, wrapped in colored blankets like a queen. In the last year, without a housemaid, the kitchen came to look like an abandoned storeroom. But father didn't complain. With his own hands he made himself dinner, always the same menu: a hard-boiled egg, a pickle, and two thick slices of bread.

At one time he used to ask: "Didn't the maid come?" But in the last year he had stopped asking. Chaos reigned in the kitchen. Mother was sunk in her own soul and didn't ask, "What did you make? How was it?" Father would go into his room without turning on the light and sink down onto the bed.

Another kind of stillness spread through the house, a cold stillness that even quieted his chatterbox mother. After an extended silence she would ask, "Has he come yet?"

"He's come."

"Where is he?"

"In his room."

And thus, with those words, her day would sometimes end. She would wrap herself up in her chair and fall asleep in her clothing.

In Theo's heart his father was forgotten. The years in the camp made him forget. However it wasn't utter oblivion. In his bosom he bore those last days with him. Crushed together in a railroad car, full of people, and afterward for some time together, until they were separated. In the end the news reached him by chance. He had been shot together with many others in the forest after an exhausting day of work.

Meanwhile Theo advanced steadily. On the hills stood abandoned horses. They raised their heads every now and then and broke out in a wild whinny. Immediately afterward they fell silent and stood in a kind of dumb astonishment. It was a broad plain, veiled with thin autumn mist, which limited visibility but felt pleasant on one's body. The thought that he was swallowing the distance on his course, section by section, and the way to his house was growing shorter and shorter, brought a new kind of joy to his heart.

After an hour of walking a woman's voice startled him: "Young fellow, what are you doing here?"

"I'm walking home."

She was a full-figured woman, and the war years were

stamped on every limb of her body. Her clothes were torn and her hands were sooty, and the two thick rolls of her legs were extended in front of her.

"Have a cup of coffee," she offered.

"Thank you very much."

"You speak German, I see."

"Correct."

She chuckled and laid her hand on her mouth, as though she had found some flaw in him.

"Why are you laughing?"

"When people talk German, it makes me laugh."

"What language do you speak?"

"Yiddish," she said and chuckled again.

The fire by her side was small, but well built, and it gave a pleasant warmth. He drank two mugs of coffee one after the other, without saying anything.

"Are you from here?" he asked afterward.

"Yes."

"And you weren't in the camps?"

"No."

Her healthy face showed she hadn't been there; it was a lean face, dark from windburn. The skin of her hands was cracked and sooty.

"Where were you all those years?"

"Here."

"You weren't afraid?"

"No."

He observed her again. If it weren't for the words she had blurted out, he would have taken her for a woodland creature. The smell of animal sweat wafted from her body.

"Where did you live in the winter?" he went on.

"In barns."

"The farmers didn't beat you?"

"No."

"You were lucky," he wanted to say. But he immediately realized that she wouldn't understand, and it would be better not to mix her up with words. She handed him a piece of peasant bread, the way one offers food to an animal. He was hungry and took the bread from her hand.

"What do you want to do?"

"Nothing." Her answer was prompt. That was clearly her intention. She wasn't seeking another life. Her face smiled again, and thick creases filled the space around her eyes. She was young but the winds had kneaded her with their hard hands and taken away the signs of her youth.

"Don't you want to go home?"

"What?"

"I'm asking whether you want to go home."

She chuckled as though she had been asked about something peculiar.

A cold morning light stood in the sky, and he wanted to get up and set out on his way. For some reason he asked, "Weren't there Germans here?"

"They were here but they left."

"I'm going home. The war is over and we have to go home."

Apparently she didn't understand the words, and she laughed. It was a loud laugh that echoed in the cold air.

"Don't you have a home? Where's your home? You weren't born here," he wanted to ask softly, but her eyes, wide and opaque, answered with great clarity: this is my house. These trees and this stream. The Germans left plenty of supplies behind them. I stashed them in a secure place. I'm not afraid of the cows. The cows know me and let me suck milk from their udders in the morning.

"I'm going," he said, stunned, and he stood up. "Thank you for the coffee."

She chuckled and placed her hand over her mouth.

Theo set out on his way. Sadness enveloped him immediately after his departure. Just a day before he had been ready to remain in this wilderness and help people. Now that desire had been wrested from him. "If people can change that way, that's a sign we are beyond hope," he said and picked up his feet. Even after he had gone some distance, the woman's image did not fade from his eyes, especially her two swollen legs, which had turned blue with cold.

As he walked he saw before him, on the crest of the hill, a group of men in two columns. They were walking innocuously, but Theo had no doubt they had followed his trail to catch him. They walked with an even pace, like people who know their way.

"I'm here," he called out, not noticing he had called out. The men on the hilltop continued walking with moderate, broad steps. That just increased his certainty that they were surrounding him on every side. Before long they stopped, took off their packs, and lit fires. "If you're looking for me, here I am. I won't hide like a mole," he called out again. He expected an answer, but no answer came. The evening spread out now, blue and high. He sat down and lit a cigarette.

From here the men didn't look threatening. On the contrary, there was a kind of moderation in their movements. Theo sat and looked at them, and the longer he sat the more he resented them. "I don't want that togetherness. I want to be alone. Isn't that clear? You can't deprive me of that choice. Now I'm free. If I've decided to become a Christian, it's because that's my faith." He spoke words he had used before.

The evening was cold and blue, and in the surrounding area no sound was heard. This deceptive silence recalled the magic of the clear autumn evenings in his distant town, the sidewalks and the church bells that used to ring at this hour. The sounds would shatter over the heads of the strolling people, bringing a kind of quiet happiness to their faces.

"You can't arrest me. I'm going home," he called out loud again. "This love stood by me all during the war. You can't take this love away from me." He could have turned to the left, climbed the hill, to confuse the pursuers, but for some reason he went to the right, returning the way he had come, and after an hour of walking he saw the monstrous woman sitting in her place and eating.

"You came back." She recognized him right away.

"Could I have a mug of coffee?" He addressed her with a pleading voice.

"Everybody takes my coffee. What will be left for me?"

"Just one mug, please." Even in the camp he hadn't begged like that.

"One mug, but no more." She acquiesced.

"Since I left you, I haven't eaten a thing." He told her the truth.

"Why didn't you get some supplies?" She scolded him. "One has to get supplies."

"I made a mistake." Something of her clumsiness clung to him.

"A person has to get supplies. The crows won't feed you." She spoke guttural Yiddish, made of the spirits of this place. He understood her.

"The coffee is excellent," he said.

She chuckled and put her hand over her mouth.

"Do a lot of people go by here?" he wanted to know.

"They go by and bother me. One of them wanted to marry me."

"What did you say to him?"

"I told him I wouldn't get married. I don't have to get married. I have everything here. Do you understand?"

Theo had often heard the word "wedding" in the camp. With many different emphases. There it was a strange-sounding word, as if it no longer belonged to people.

He sensed that if he asked for another mug she would refuse. He put his hands out over the fire, and the heat flowed into his tattered coat. "It's warm here," he said.

"I warm myself all day long. At night I light two fires. There are plenty of twigs around." Only now did he notice that her big body gave the impression of overflowing from inside her. "She apparently can't walk on her legs anymore, so she crawls on all fours." The thought passed through his brain.

"Aren't you afraid?" he asked for some reason.

"I'm not afraid. The peasants are good to me and don't do me any harm. They don't curse me. And I don't curse them."

"Give me another mug." He reached the mug out to her.

He expected her to refuse, but she said, "I'll give you some this time. But don't ask for any more. I don't like it when people ask for too much. You have to get supplies." She poured coffee for him, and he drank. His few words went mute within him. He wanted to lay his head on the stump and shut his eyes. But he gathered his strength and overcame his weakness, setting forth on his way. She didn't ask why or where. As though he were an abandoned animal.

VIII

Now the pursuers were marching along the horizon, in two columns, like soldiers. In the distance they looked like a well-knit group, with no slackers. It was clear: they wouldn't let him go. Theo sat down and followed them tensely with his eyes. Now he imagined to himself how they would trap him and how they would throw him into a shallow puddle and beat him with boards. "I won't beg, and I won't crawl on my knees. I'll stand with my back straight as long as my soul is within me," he decided then and there, but in his heart he knew that taller men than he, sturdier men than he, had been subdued with clubs. Pain, in the end, overcomes even the strongest will. He knew that and it made him angry. Later he realized there weren't so many of them, not more than ten, but in any case he couldn't get that fear out of his heart, that they were many and would cut him off. He advanced. The trail was well worn, and at its sides metal spools, containers, and boxes were scattered, the objects that any retreating army throws from its vehicles.

"Coffee. A cup of hot coffee," he called out again in his mother's voice. Between one train and another, on the way to one of the churches or on the way back, she would suddenly be struck with the desire for a cup of coffee. She used to love a snifter of cognac, a fine cigarette, but they were luxuries one could forgo. Without coffee the chills gripped her body. "A cup of coffee. Why isn't there a cup of coffee? This is a settlement, not the wilderness. A buffet without coffee? What good will lemonade do us?" He remembered that voice in all his fibers. He also remembered her sigh of relief after they were finally seated in a village inn, with a glass of cognac at her side, and a cigarette. Those smells accompanied him on every trip. Once she said, "Mama can't manage without a cup of coffee. Even in the world to come she'll need a cup of coffee. That's a great weakness, but you forgive me, don't you?"

Her faith in the next world was strong. She spoke about it with simplicity, as when she said, "Don't worry, dear. This dreary day is only an illusion. We're slowly sailing on to another world. Believe me."

"Where is it?" he would ask her when he was still a boy.

"Beyond the mountains. A distance of thirty miles, no more." Her smile would not be long in coming.

In high school he no longer asked. He listened to her in amazement. Her belief in the next world grew stronger. Once, after they had gone to a Bach concert, she said to him, "We just spent a full hour in the world to come. Marvelous. Too bad we were driven away from there. But I'm not worried, my dear. For we're sailing there." At the Church of Saint

Paul, when he was in the eighth grade, she said, "From now on don't miss any of the concerts at the Church of Saint Paul. This is the secret meeting place of all the lovers."

In the last year, on leave from the sanatorium, she would describe the world to come like a vast hall, and all along it choruses were singing Bach cantatas. At the end they served French cognac and coffee in thin porcelain cups. All her descriptions would finally bring her to the coffee counter. As though the world had only been created to ply people with fine coffee. So much for the next world. Regarding the here below, she was in touch with a great many objects. Not just with the pillows and blankets in which she wrapped herself in the living room. And not just the blue sofa she loved to lie on in the late morning. Near the lake at Hofheim she told him, "The water isn't black, it's only hiding." Immediately she broke out in loud laughter. And once on their way back, on the bridge, she spoke in amazement: "I have stepped upon you before, bridge. You don't remember. How could you remember? But I remember. You forget. You're forgetful by nature." When she parted from them and took her last journey, she said: "Good-bye, children, good-bye, house. We shall see each other very soon."

While he was walking, sure there was no one around him, he saw a woman with a girl at her side, two meager parcels, and a tall birch tree, a leafless skeleton. "My name is Theo." He introduced himself. The woman was startled, hugged the girl with both arms, and didn't utter a word. "Camp eight," Theo added, "and now I'm on my way home." These details didn't erase the fear from the mother's face. Her hands trembled.

"I'll gather some leaves and start a fire. It's cold in the

evening," he said, but his helpfulness didn't calm the woman's fears. "Leave us alone," her eyes spoke. "We don't need help."

"What are you afraid of? I'm a refugee too. If we don't help each other, who will help us?" He spoke, but he immediately sensed that he shouldn't have spoken in that way.

When she didn't respond he said, "If my presence disturbs you, I'll go my way. I'm headed straight for the Austrian border." That remark also failed to calm the women's fears. They clung to their places and didn't utter a word.

"I don't have any supplies," Theo added. "I can leave you a pack of cigarettes. I myself smoke a lot and know how hard it is to be without cigarettes." He immediately took a pack of cigarettes out of his pocket and laid it on the ground.

"Thanks." The woman let a word out of her mouth.

"Why are you so frightened?"

The woman took a cigarette from the pack, lit it, and said, "Yesterday a refugee went by here, a young man of your age, and he robbed us. We didn't have many supplies, but he took everything. He even took my daughter's jacket. You won't beat us?"

"Perish the thought," said Theo.

"Why do you want to help us?" The woman surprised him.

"I feel obligated to." He recovered his thoughts. "A person must help others."

The woman didn't understand. That explanation only intensified her suspicion, and she said weakly, "Don't worry. We'll manage."

"I won't burden you. I'm healthy. I'll just bring some twigs, and I'll be on my way." He spoke in a voice that wasn't his own.

"We've had something to drink. We're not thirsty or hungry. Don't bother. You're probably in a hurry."

"How do you know?"

"Your face says so."

"If I gather a few twigs and make a fire, that won't disturb you. I won't linger, and I won't bother you. Why shouldn't we help each other? We're humans, after all. If we don't help each other, who'll help us?"

"How can I explain to you?" said the woman, and it was clear she was afraid to tell the truth.

Theo got up and, without saying anything, went to gather twigs. The woman observed him tensely. Before long the fire was giving heat. The woman apparently regretted her blunt words and said, "There are bad refugees too. I'm very scared of them." Her face was completely exposed, a face reddened and scuffed by the cold wind. Her daughter's face too was wizened by the wind. She was a girl of about fifteen; her eyes were sunken in their sockets and peered out with a kind of cold surprise. Theo brought water from the stream and the woman put a pot on the burning twigs. "We had a lot of supplies, cans of food, lots of sugar and flour. That evil man took everything."

"I'll bring some for you. At the side of the road there are lots of supplies."

"There's no need," the woman hurriedly answered. "A person should take care of himself and not be a burden. One mustn't count on other people."

"We must help one another. After all, we're human beings."

"You're right." She retreated slightly.

"I don't intend to stay here. I'll have a drink and go. You have nothing to fear."

"God will not forgive that wicked man who plundered all our supplies. The day will come when he'll have to account for his deeds." The woman spoke in the tones people used before the war. "Why are you walking alone?"

"I want to be by myself." Theo remembered that sentence in its entirety.

"I have nobody left in the world. Of my whole family only my daughter remains to me. We were in camp ten. You certainly know what that means."

"I do," Theo said and bent his head. Later he whispered, "I'll get going. Maybe I'll find some supplies."

"Don't bother. We'll manage," said the woman. "Go on your way, and we'll go to our fate."

Theo didn't respond to that rejection and went on. At the sides of the trail lay packages of clothing, some packs that had been saved from the camps, but nothing to eat. He walked farther but found nothing. The prolonged search wearied his legs, and when the sun set he sank down and fell asleep where he was.

The next day fortune favored him, and not far from the path he found cans of food, a crate of biscuits, and a container of coffee. It was clear by the way they were scattered that they had been abandoned in flight. The booty made Theo happy, and he immediately turned back.

He found the women where he had left them, curled up with each other. The fire had died down. When they noticed him they were startled. The mother couldn't control her voice and said, "What are you doing here?"

"I found some supplies. Why don't we make some breakfast?"

"Mama"—the girl clung to her mother—"I'm frightened."

"You have nothing to be afraid of. This man won't do us any harm." The woman spoke hoarsely.

"Let's make a cup of coffee. A person needs a cup of coffee in the morning." The voice of former days returned to him. The desire for action, which had been suppressed in him for many days, surged up from inside him. His hands, which were still frozen with the chill of the night, immediately did what was required of them. Before long fire broke out from the thin splinters of wood. The mother tried to tell her daughter, "You see, there's nothing to be afraid of," but the daughter didn't hear her voice. She was curled up next to her like a frightened animal.

"Where are you from?" asked the woman surprisingly.

"From Baden-bei-Wien," Theo answered immediately, pleased she had finally spoken to him.

"My parents used to travel to Baden-bei-Wien, but I never went there," said the woman, smiling, as though the words had touched the roots of her dormant memory. Immediately she added: "A beautiful town."

"A small city, but a very beautiful one." Theo quickly told her, "In Baden-bei-Wien I finished my secondary studies. If it weren't for the war, I would have completed three years of university by now."

"What were you intending to study?"

"Art history."

"Strange," said the woman. Her face changed and took on an old-time softness. "The Jews usually tended toward practical subjects. Unless I am mistaken?" A smile bloomed on her lips, as though the words she had spoken were not her own.

"Mama wanted me to study music. She wasn't a musician, but she loved music a lot. Everything went wrong."

"True," said the woman, and a kind of surprise spread out on her forehead. "Everything went wrong. Nothing is in the right place anymore." The daughter grasped her mug with both hands. The skin of her hands had wide cracks, and a kind of moist redness showed inside the cracks. Theo looked carefully at her small hands and said, "Why don't you eat some biscuits." The daughter didn't respond, and Theo was sorry he had spoken to her without her mother's permission. The mother sensed the approaching disaster, and she hugged her. A moment later the daughter burst out crying. The mother said, "She's cold, very cold. When she's cold, she cries."

Theo got up and went to gather wood. On the way he found two dry branches and immediately broke them into splinters with his hands. Once again the fire gave off heat, and the mother labored to console the daughter with words in Hungarian, which Theo couldn't understand. "A day ago, not far from here, I saw a package of halvah. I was stupid and didn't pick it up." Theo spoke to himself. The mother didn't respond. She tried to calm her daughter. The daughter didn't cry anymore. She was trembling.

Theo sensed that the two women wanted only one thing: for him to go away. The mother's face said, "Leave us alone. Let us be. Why are you being cruel? You're worse than the thief who robbed us." Theo heard that silent plea and said, "I'm going. I didn't mean any harm. But if I'm disturbing you, I'll go. Just give me a moment, and I'll go."

"Thanks," said the woman. "Don't worry. We'll get by. You understand that." An old kind of beauty and goodness shone in her big eyes.

"I can help you. I'm healthy." Theo went back to his old ways.

"You can't help us." The woman's answer was clear and unequivocal.

"I'll go," he said.

The woman didn't detain him. She expected him to leave and go off on his way. But for some reason he stood there, his legs planted in the earth, like an animal that has been rebuked.

The daylight waned and it was as though the red, rough skin was sloughed off the woman's forehead, and clear skin, the skin from before the war, peeked out from between the thin folds with a homey kind of gleam. "No one likes me anymore." The thought passed through his mind, and he immediately went out to gather twigs.

Afterward he sat by the fire and drank two mugs of coffee. The woman didn't offer him biscuits, and he didn't take any. The daughter folded herself up and fell asleep where she was.

"You're afraid of me."

"I'm not," the woman answered immediately, "but my daughter is."

"She's afraid of me?"

"Men frighten her."

"In the morning I'll be on my way."

"Pardon me," said the woman, bending her head.

Before long the daughter woke up and burst into tears. Her mother hugged her to her bosom and the weeping increased. Now he saw her face clearly: about fifteen years old. The weeping narrowed her face. She dug her fingers into the ground as though they were going to drag her away. "Why don't you go away?" The woman fastened him with her gaze. An animal phosphorescence was in her eyes.

Theo wanted to get up, but his legs were shackled with

fatigue. For a long time the daughter's bitter weeping trickled into his ears. Fatigue overcame his entire body, and before long he sank down asleep.

When he woke up the sun was in the sky, the fire still glowed. The two women had gone away, taking their belongings. "Where am I?" Theo asked, as though the ground had been snatched away from under his feet.

Later he fanned up the fire to make at least a cup of coffee for himself. But when he touched the can his mother's face floated up before him. In his last year of high school, when he was on his way to a mathematics examination, she had told him: "Don't worry. I'll defend you. You have nothing to fear. I'll be with you everywhere."

IX

THE NEXT MORNING he headed north. The trail was wide and clear, and at one bend a truck lay on its side. The snout covering the motor pointed upward, giving the giant box a clumsy look. Theo stared at the body of the truck for a moment, and it immediately occurred to him that he would find supplies inside.

All around crates, containers, and vegetables were scattered. Evidently these supplies had just been thrown away a few days ago, during the retreat. For a moment the place looked like a picnic ground where raucous vacationers had littered the landscape. He remembered vandalized picnic areas from his childhood. His mother would stand there, angrily saying, "Savages. The world is full of savages. See what they've done to this marvelous place. They've wounded it."

Not a sound was heard around him. He lit a fire and collected vegetables for a meal. He had not eaten a fresh vegetable since the beginning of the war, and here, to his surprise, he found crates of onions, cabbages, and radishes. He remembered the woman and her daughter who had slipped away from him in the middle of the night. For some reason it seemed to him they were watching from behind a tree. It made him angry that they had pushed away the hand he had extended. Now he saw the skin of the older woman's face very clearly: thick, rough skin.

The heavy meal calmed him down somewhat. He sat by the fire and drank mug after mug of coffee. The evening fell silently on the hills opposite, and the shadows grew thicker. While he was sitting there and watching, forgotten and lost, a crack opened in the silence. He heard the voice of his mother talking to him. "Why don't we go to Salzburg? The time has come to travel to Salzburg." Salzburg, one of her hidden desires. She would pronounce the name in many tones. While he was still a boy she had dragged him to Salzburg in the winter. It was a harsh winter, and the roads were blocked. For three full days they inched along. Finally they reached an abandoned railroad station at night. His mother was upset and confused, and in her agitation she entered a workers' bar and drank a few glasses of cognac. She joked with the owner and his few guests. The owner sized her up quickly and called her "our singer." The nickname apparently flattered her, and she agreed to sing some folksongs. Fortunately they managed to catch the midnight train, and equally fortunately the snow stopped. They arrived home the next morning with no further delay. His frightened father opened the door and asked: "Dear God, where were you?"

"In Salzburg," she answered in a loud, festive voice.

"Madness!" His father didn't restrain his voice.

When Theo was a junior in high school, once again her desire for Salzburg flared up, this time with a vengeance. "We have to get to Salzburg soon." There was no money. Theo tried to stand by his father. By that time they had already sold their two sets of cutlery, their silver platters, and the carpets. Cold nakedness dwelled in the living room. But that excuse didn't count for her. "The Salzburg festival is about to begin, and we must get there right away."

"How? We haven't got any money."

"Papa is a miser. He must pay for this trip. It's an important trip. You only take a trip like this once in your life."

"Papa's in financial trouble. Why can't you understand?"

"Don't say financial trouble. There are things more important than financial trouble."

March was cold, and his mother sat in the living room wrapped in two blankets and an old fur coat. But her eyes were wide awake and sharp, and she was firm in her decision: "To Salzburg. Tomorrow I'm selling my jewels, and we'll have plenty of cash." She had forgotten that they had already sold her jewels, and what was left in her jewel box was cheap costume jewelry.

In the evening she fell upon her husband and called him an incorrigible miser. His father stood, stunned, in the kitchen, and didn't utter a word. She rose from her armchair and swung her arms up into the air, announcing: "No one is going to do me favors anymore. I'll take my savings out of the bank, and from now on everything will be at my expense." She had forgotten that her bank account had long since been closed. They were living from hand to mouth.

Several times she dressed in her winter clothes and announced, "I'm going on a trip." Theo was helpless. He tried in vain to dissuade her. She insisted: "We must get to Salzburg. There pure streams of music flow. Only someone who has been to Salzburg and drunk in those pure tones knows what music is. Only there can one be purified. We must be purified. Why are you so stubborn? Is it so hard to understand?" In the end the hail decided for them. It was a heavy, dirty hail that darkened the sky and cast a melancholy spell on his mother. She took off her coat and sank down on the sofa in tears.

The next day the sky cleared. Her tears were forgotten, and she put on her coat, announcing, "I'm setting out."

"Mama, we haven't got any money." Theo spoke gently.

"We'll go by foot. One makes pilgrimages to holy places by foot, doesn't one?"

"In the spring we'll have money and we'll take the train."

"You're talking like Papa. You mustn't talk to me like Papa."

He didn't know how right she was. That year the snow fell all during May. She poured her anger out on the stove, which didn't heat the house or her feet. Theo tried to distract her, but nothing worked; the Salzburg festival couldn't be erased from her mind. She spoke of the urgent need to detach herself from earthly bonds and see the world with new and refreshed eyes, to climb up to high lookout points and view precious sights. "Wings, my dear. Without wings, my dear, we scuffle about like hens in the farmyard. Mozart will give me wings, and Bach will open up the gates of light for us." That was her true plan.

At that time Theo was up to his ears in exams. The Latin teacher had it in for him. In one of his lessons the teacher expressed his opinion: Theo Braun indeed had a sharp mind, but it wasn't always clear. Clarity was more important than a sharp wit. Theo wanted to prove to that anti-Semite that his judgment was malicious and distorted. He prepared for all his tests thoroughly.

His mother would sit in the living room and revile all the wicked people who prevented her from going out on trips and giving herself over to pure music, but most of her anger was directed at her husband. She called him a miser who would certainly pay for his stinginess.

At that time she took up a new habit: notes. She would write notes and leave them in every corner of the house. They were mostly instructions to the maid, who no longer was working for them, and reprimands to her husband for his disgraceful behavior.

In one of her notes she wrote, "Theo, I order you to travel to Salzburg. You must overcome all obstacles and hesitations, take courage, and, with the first express, set out on your way. Mozart will give you wings. You can take off to wherever you wish. Your loving mother." In a textbook he found a yellow piece of paper on which she had written, "Pay no attention to slanderers. Don't be afraid. God is with us. Make a pilgrimage to Salzburg, and there you should seek the lookout point known as the Eagle's Nest. From that spot you can take off. You musn't be buried in the provinces. The provinces devour their inhabitants. Free yourself of all bonds."

At that time her pen never left her hands. She would plant notes in strange places. A woman, one of his father's distant relations, used to come once a week to tidy the house a little. She would gather up all the notes and put them on the buffet. "Child, read what your mother wrote to you," she would say when Theo got home from school. Then, of course, Theo didn't know they were precious testaments that had to be read with care. The notes aroused a kind of painful embarrassment in him.

One evening, upon returning from a long day of studies, he found the woman reading one of the notes and laughing. Without thinking he raised his voice at her and shouted, "Get out of here. You're a sneak!" In great alarm, without saying a word, she fled for her life as if from a burning house.

From then on no stranger entered their home. His mother continued writing notes and hiding them in every corner of the house. She didn't forget the Salzburg festival. She spoke about the world of freedom for which one must prepare with diligence, and without any neglect. The word "neglect" was frequently repeated in her notes, a word she didn't usually use. At that time Theo's attention grew somewhat fainter. He did listen to her, but not attentively. That apparently disturbed her; perhaps she suspected her beloved son no longer believed in her visions.

One morning she opened the window and publicly announced: "The world of freedom is on its way. No one can keep us from that longed-for meeting." Theo pleaded with her, using all the words in his possession, but nothing worked. Seized by enthusiasm and a sense of mission she stood at the window and shouted: "The world of freedom is on its way, bringing an end to all suffering." So that her words would not only be heard, but also seen, she removed her clothes and stood naked at the open window. Theo struggled with her for a long time. She was obstinate and strong-willed. She grasped the windowsill and wouldn't let go. Even after he had detached her from the window she kept shouting insults. She called her husband a cold-blooded murderer.

In the evening, when two attendants came to take her to the sanatorium, to his surprise she was quiet and polite. She spoke to them like a matron to her servants, she was in a good mood, and offered them a drink. They looked at her closely as a cunning smile twisted her lips. They didn't rush her, and she dressed and made up her face without hurrying. The blue silk dress suited her wonderfully. For a moment it seemed as though she were going out to an exhibit at the museum. The attendants, two sturdy men, sat at the table and smoked pipes, not making any comment. They had apparently expected shouts and abuse, but his mother's behavior was quiet and unexceptional. She didn't ask where she was going, and the attendants didn't bother to inform her.

"I'll try to be back soon," she announced, like someone harboring a secret. At the door a long automobile was waiting for her, but not a luxurious one. Once it had been used to deliver food, and now it transported patients to the sanatorium. When the car went on its way she stuck her right hand out through the barred window and waved good-bye, as in former times, when she was going to the opera.

Late at night his father burst into tears, a stifled weeping that sounded like a whimper. Theo lit the light in the corridor and called from a distance: "Papa."

"What?" his voice was heard from within.

"Don't you feel well?"

"Everything's fine, Theo."

"Can I do anything for you?"

"Everything's fine. There's nothing to worry about." Theo turned off the light in the hallway, and darkness filled the room.

X

AT NIGHT RAIN FELL, and Theo took shelter in the cabin of the truck. The cabin had a comfortable seat, two drawers full of sweets, and the smell of tobacco, reminding him of old cafés saturated with smoke. He had barely laid his body on the upholstery before he fell asleep.

He slept for many hours, a dreamless sleep which bore him with great lightness on soft and pliant waves. When he woke up it seemed to him that a primus stove was burning nearby. A full, cold sun shone high in the sky. The thought that in a little while he would have a mug full of coffee in his hand and a piece of chocolate roused him from his slumber completely. He stood erect. It was as though at night he had discovered that his guilt was not great, and he could stand at his full height without embarrassment.

With their magic the coffee and chocolate restored distant times to him, his high school years. In the last year of high

school they used to go to Vienna in groups to enjoy themselves in one of the better-known whorehouses. On one of
those trips he ended up with a coarse, sturdy whore who
called him Bobby, and after they were finished she turned her
back on him like a beast.

That memory brought a smile to his lips, as though it
wasn't something that had happened to him. He remembered the entrance, or rather the entrance stairs, the two
windows sealed with heavy curtains, the whores in transparent pink dresses. The boy who served drinks used to pass by
them and pinch them with pleasure. The perfume and the
coarse language, the banknotes that the porter used to gather
greedily. At the end, the darkness next to the exit stairs, rough
wooden stairs.

But in the meantime reality reasserted itself. The pursuers,
it turned out, hadn't forgotten him. They were advancing in
a tight-knit group on the horizon. Though they didn't make a
sound, it seemed as though they were singing. There was
determination in their steps.

"I want to be alone," Theo shouted out loud and immediately understood that that wasn't a suitable answer to their
determined marching. They were approaching for good reasons of their own: the unforgiven shove.

Now, somehow, his guilt seemed clearer to him. He was
prepared to stand up and defend himself, and he even had his
opening sentence on his lips: "I am guilty, but of no wrongdo-
ing." He smiled to himself for finding that sentence, but
before long he realized that it was self-contradictory.

While he was sipping his coffee, a tall man approached
him. From a distance he seemed like a vacationer who had
gone for a stroll in the fields. When he stood nearby there was

no doubt: a survivor. Theo was happy to have him there and immediately offered him a cup of coffee.

"Gladly," said the man with gratitude.

"Where are you heading, if I may ask?"

"To Budapest. Four hundred miles, if I'm not mistaken."

"Are you making the trip by yourself?" Theo examined him.

"It's a personal matter," the man said without further explanation. It had been years since Theo had heard the expression "a personal matter." In the camps people hadn't used it. Now when he heard it again for the first time, he was pleased at this sudden revelation. He handed the man a cup of coffee and a handful of sweet biscuits.

"All kinds of lovely things are happening to me on this road," the man confessed.

"Lovely?" Theo was surprised.

"Yes, my young friend. At every turn people offer me affection, food, and drink."

The man seemed to be about fifty years old, Theo's father's age. A kind of spirituality was carved on his forehead, and it was clear that before the war he had been close to books, like Theo's father, but the rest of his face was seared with wind and cold. His lips turned down, and the creases along his face were broad and deep.

The man swallowed his coffee and Theo went to make him another mug. After days of fear, isolation, and people who hadn't received him kindly, he was glad to have found a man whose face was familiar. His accent was clear, and his language was Theo's own: Viennese.

"And where are you headed?" the man asked softly.

"To the city of my birth, Baden-bei-Wien."

A smile crossed the man's face, as though a distant memory had arisen within him. He said, "In my childhood I went there once, but I don't remember a thing about it." The way he spoke again evoked the image of Theo's father—his father before he shut himself off, before he became mute, from the days when he would still exchange complete sentences with his wife and son.

"I'm glad I met you. It's hard for me in the company of the refugees. They all talk Yiddish," Theo confessed.

"I learned Yiddish in the camps."

"And you speak it fluently?"

"I acquired the language by dint of hard effort. In our home it was absolutely forbidden."

"I have a kind of aversion to that language." Theo didn't hide the truth from him.

"At first I also had a kind of aversion. It was hard for me to absorb the words, but I got used to it."

"I tried too, but all my attempts were fruitless. My ears simply don't hear the language."

"Gradually one learns to love it. Now I don't feel any barrier. As though it were my mother tongue."

"It's hard for me to understand that," Theo said and fell silent.

After a few moments of silence he said, "I'm going back to my hometown. One must return to one's hometown. I have no other city in the world."

"I'm going back to Budapest, my parents' city," said the man, and a kind of surprise was aroused in his eyes. "I don't know what's awaiting me there. I feel that I must go back there."

"Do you expect to find your parents?"

"They perished. I know that for a certainty. I owe you a small explanation. Before the deportation my wife and I converted from our fathers' faith. In our great stupidity we believed that conversion would save us. My parents never forgave me. They weren't religious, but still they asked me not to convert."

"Strange," said Theo. "I'm going back to my hometown in order to convert. That was my mother's wish, it seems to me. I feel that it's not quite right, but still I can't do anything else."

"*Now* you're going to do that?"

"My mother loved the church to the depths of her soul. You should know that my mother was an unusual woman."

"I," said the man, "did what I did for selfish reasons. I thought it would save me."

"My mother was a believing woman."

"And your father?"

"I don't know. I never talked about it with him. He was a closed man and didn't speak much about his beliefs. He had a large bookshop, but my mother was strongly drawn to the church. My father and mother were divorced before the deportations."

The man received Theo's hastily spoken words without comment. A kind of dark gloom suddenly showed on his forehead. The words he wanted to say were blocked in his mouth. He said only this: "Please give me another mug of coffee. I would be very grateful." Theo felt a kind of warm closeness toward the man, as though he had brought the key to his secret with him. "I don't know what to tell you," the man finally said. "I really mustn't tell you. I'm going back to Budapest to beg my parents' forgiveness. Their forgiveness is very important."

"You're a believer, I see."

"The camp made me into a believer. The camp opened my eyes and granted me the good fortune of meeting many wonderful people. Actually, I wouldn't exactly call myself a believer, but I feel that I have received some precious pledge from them. Do you understand me? We were together and we helped each other. There was a kind of radiance. We were frightened. We were very frightened, but there was a strong feeling of togetherness. My life before the war, may God forgive me, was narrow."

"Didn't the Ukrainians beat you?"

"They beat us, but our souls refused to surrender. We helped one another. We were proud of every day that passed."

"Do you hate me?" Theo's question was a surprise.

"What are you talking about? How could I hate you? I myself am as full of sins as a pomegranate is full of seeds. My brothers did far more for me than I was worthy of. They took me in as though I had been their brother from time immemorial. No one reproached me for converting."

"A strong feeling is leading me home." Theo bared his soul.

"If a strong feeling is guiding you, you must obey it."

But that very affirmation weakened Theo's resolve. Once again he was no longer sure he was doing the right thing. Perhaps it was because he no longer saw his mother, leaning on the window and observing the members of the choir on their way to the church. The sight of his house and the city were as though suddenly wrapped in thick fog.

For a long while they sat without exchanging a word. Before Theo's eyes flashed the road he had taken since the liberation. Now it appeared to him like a narrow, tight passageway whose opening grew ever thinner.

Meanwhile the stranger was metamorphosed into his father. The way he leaned on the package, the hands, the stooping back that indicated the acceptance of the yoke and resignation. He had become so like his father, that it seemed to Theo he was about to get up and put on his coat and go out for his day's work in the bookstore.

"The people we lost are grasping all those who survived." The thought passed through Theo's mind. The man raised his head and said, "If your feeling tells you to return to your hometown, you should do so. One must honor one's feeling."

"Thank you." Theo tried to express his gratitude.

"I'm heading straight to Budapest. That emotion has been pulling me along for a month now. My forefathers came from there. I want to learn how to pray from them. I have a need for prayer. Do you understand me?"

"I," answered Theo, "have never prayed in my life. But I loved to see how my mother sat at the window, greeting the members of the choir and afterward standing and listening to the music flowing from the church. We would go from church to church to hear music. All during the war the music was within me. Now I'm afraid to lose it."

"It's yours. No one can take it from you."

"I am so frightened of being left without music." Theo raised his voice.

"The body can be murdered, but not the soul. That is what we learned in the past three years."

"Do you believe in the immortality of the soul?"

"I no longer feel loneliness."

Later they pored over Theo's maps. He had two military maps of a very limited area. One could merely guess what was beyond it.

"What did you do before the war?" Theo asked for some reason.

"I was a violinist."

"My father also played the violin for many years, but he stopped. He wasn't satisfied with his playing."

"I was the concertmaster of a local orchestra. I have no desire to return to the instrument."

"Nor to sing in the synagogue?"

"Jewish prayer is the essence of simplicity. One takes a prayerbook in his hands and prays."

"You've given up music?"

"Our camp was full of classical music. The commander of the camp was mad about Mozart."

Toward evening the man rose to his feet and said, "Thank you for the hospitality. I must move along."

"It's late. Why not sleep in the cabin of the truck?" Theo tried to detain him.

"I must move along. I have quite a long way."

"What do you intend to do?" he asked again.

"In the future I intend to work with my hands. Such is the work I need, and no other."

Theo didn't offer to join the man. In his bones he knew that the man wanted to be alone.

That night Theo saw his father very clearly, sitting at the table and eating his frugal meal. For a moment he wanted to go over and ask him how the trip had been, but his father was so deeply immersed in himself that Theo didn't dare. The next morning as well, when he woke from his sleep, the vision of his father didn't fade, as though he had sat by his side all that time.

XI

THE NEXT DAY Theo set out on his way. On the hills across from him the pursuers advanced with measured, uniform steps. They seemed content, and the packs on their backs fit them. Though there were no hostile signs, it was clear to Theo that they were following him closely. That knowledge didn't frighten him. He strode along on a line parallel to their hillcrest at a distance of one mile.

On the sides of the road, beneath the low trees, the refugees lay scattered about. Occasionally a child would emerge from the thicket, look about, and disappear from sight. The people sat at a distance from each other, wrapped in the shadows of the trees, as if after a bad argument. Theo went by them, and no one asked any questions.

Before they had been happy, now they were neglected; an evil thought passed through Theo's mind. Theo knew that he too, until a few days ago, had been firm in his resolve not to deviate from his course; now he had come back to everyone. Thirst for a mug of coffee tormented him silently, but no one offered him any. In fact there weren't any campfires, only two miserable blazes that sent up thick, dark, unpleasant smoke. "They won't leave me alone. What do they want from me?" The thoughts passed through his mind. Strange, the pursuers didn't occupy him, but rather these, the stragglers, who lay under the low trees and didn't demand anything from anyone.

"Can I have a mug of coffee?" he finally asked one of the people sitting there.

"I have no coffee. I don't have anything. I lit the fire to warm the air. But this fire is colder than ice."

"Where can one get something to drink?" Theo addressed him as though the man owed him something.

"I would gladly give you something, but I don't have a thing."

Now he noticed: the man was very similar to his Uncle Karl, his father's older brother, a watchmaker. For years the members of the family had tried to rescue him from that miserable profession, but those efforts ended in failure. He remained stuck in his place, a bachelor, lacking everything. Finally he converted and received a small annuity from the church. The deportations didn't spare him either, and in the last transport he was brought to the railroad station. All the way to the station and even afterward he was gay and joked about all the jobs he'd had during his lifetime; he sang cantorial selections, imitated a suburban priest, helped people drag their packages, and he died one cold winter night.

"Where are you headed?" asked the man, with Uncle Karl's voice.

"Home," answered Theo without hesitation.

"It's lovely to return home."

"Why lovely?" Theo asked angrily.

"I said lovely. What else can be added? To add would only take away, isn't that what they used to say?"

Uncle Karl, one of the dearest people from his childhood, a man without melancholy, had a gaiety that sometimes sounded like melancholy. In fact he only wanted to make people feel good. He met no success, and he became a buffoon. He developed that trait, and over the years he exaggerated it. The church, of course, didn't change his character. He didn't go there often. He would imitate the suburban priest any chance he got. But the essence of his character found expression only in the camp. Everything good in him welled up. And when he died, everyone in the shed wept, as though a light had been taken away.

"May I sit for a while?" Theo asked.

"Gladly. But what good will it do you to sit? I have nothing. Everyone else got supplies, but I just didn't have my wits about me. I'm stuck without anything. I don't know how to live. It's my fault."

"There are plenty of supplies, all over." Theo tried to console him.

"Not for me, friend. The others have grazed everything bare. They didn't leave a thing." Indeed it was Uncle Karl's voice, but not his tone. The tone had changed completely. Now nothing was left in his strains except resentment and despair.

"It's good you have faith. Good you're returning home. I no longer have the strength for that." Now another voice was mingled with his, also a familiar one, but Theo couldn't identify it. He sat by the man's side for a short while, and the longer he sat, the more he felt that the despair laid up in the man's body was flowing into him in a mighty stream. Theo rose and said, "I'm setting out." The man didn't call him back. Theo walked away, and the man watched him as he disappeared into the distance. On all sides faces stared at him, mute faces, reminding him of sights from past years: the small Hapsburg park where old people used to sit in the autumn, with salesgirls and a few wild young idlers. Even the whore, Hilda, whom every boy in high school had patronized at least once. He imagined he saw that half-Jewish woman next to one of the trees. "I'm going home, ladies and gentlemen," he wanted to call out loud. "You can sit here as long as you want, but I'm going home. I have a home. Can't you understand that? Is there any need to waste words and explain it all?"

"Do you have a cigarette?" A man addressed him.

"With pleasure," said Theo.

"I thank you from the bottom of my heart," the man said, turning his back.

At a narrow place in the road a woman stood next to a fire and called out loud: "Coffee, ladies and gentlemen. We need a hot drink." She was a woman of about fifty, sturdily built, and at first glance it appeared she was offering her wares as in a country fair. Theo was about to walk by her. "My young friend, why not have a mug of coffee?" The woman stopped him with a motherly voice.

"Thank you." It had been years since he'd heard such a voice.

"Have many people been here?"

"No, my dear, very few. Today there has been no one.

You're the first. This is an out-of-the-way place. I should have moved on. It's hard to drag all these sacks."

It was a spacious tent, made of empty bags sewn together and a few military tarpaulins stretched on ropes at the foot of the trees. Inside the tent, sacks were arranged with a strange tidiness, like grocery stores in former times, next to tables made of thick boards.

"I got everything ready. I'm ready to receive people."

"And people come?"

"Very few. It's important to eat, I tell them. It's important to drink. Not only for our own sakes, but for the sake of future generations. We must eat and drink." A kind of simplicity was in her voice, like a household servant with no family of her own, entirely devoted to her employers.

"You gathered all that?"

"With my own hands. I was sure that many people would come. People need to eat and gain their strength. For years they didn't eat or drink. I have clean, unspoiled supplies. Hundreds of people could sit here and rest and eat. Why hurry?"

"A person has to take care of himself," Theo said for some reason.

"I, my dear, no longer need to be concerned. My children already live in the world of truth, and now I am going to them. I have another stretch of road to walk. And where are you from, my dear?"

"From Baden-bei-Wien."

"I've heard a lot about that town. They say it's a pretty town. I won't ask you any more. One mustn't ask. I've already learned not to ask. But sometimes a question comes up by itself. I very much regret it."

"You may ask. I'll answer you gladly."

"People ask me, why don't you leave this place and move on? Everybody is moving on and going home. I answer them quite simply: here I can serve people coffee and sandwiches. People haven't had anything to drink for years. They've worked like slaves and they've been abused. Every one of us saw how they were abused. Now they're very thirsty. I'm glad I am able to prepare sandwiches for them. It's very easy. Nothing could be easier."

"Don't you want to go back to your hometown?"

"My place is here, my dear. Everyone has a place, and this place was allotted to me. I'm not complaining anymore. This isn't a bad place. If I put in a stove it will be warm in the winter. I've spent two winters outdoors. I'm used to the cold. Cold doesn't affect me."

"I'm going back to my hometown." Theo didn't hide his destination from her.

"A man's wish is his fate. I won't tell anyone what to do. At one time I forbade my younger sister to go to America. I was sure I was doing the intelligent thing. See what I've done to my good sister. See what I did to my two beautiful daughters. I'll never forgive myself. Now I don't tell anybody anything. Even something trivial. Drink a cup of coffee, take a sandwich. I have plenty of supplies. Eight sacks of flour. I could make bread for a regiment. But people aren't coming to my tent. You must tell them that there's everything here. Anyone who's hungry may come and eat. I even have cans of sardines. I don't understand why they don't come here. Why are they in a hurry? Is my food bad? Why are they shunning my tent?"

"Soon they'll come. A lot of people will come," Theo said to console her.

"If you meet people on the way, send them here. With your

own eyes you've seen what I have. I'm not leaving this place. I'll be here forever."

"I'll send them," he promised.

"Thank you, my dear."

"And you'll never leave this area?"

"No, my dear. Here in this forest all my dear ones lie. Who will watch over them?"

That simplicity panicked Theo into motion.

"I'm moving on," he said.

"I don't want to detain you. One mustn't detain someone while he has momentum. Now he knows what he wants. Who knows what tomorrow will bring? I don't wish to detain you. You have a long way."

Just as he left the narrow place, he discovered the file of marchers on the line of the hillcrests. They strode in pairs like soldiers. One could hear the rhythmic crunch of their boots. The hills grew taller and taller, and as he advanced they loomed over him. Another shade of green, thick, the green of abundant water, spread over the slopes. Moist silence permeated the narrow path. "I'll sit for a moment and smoke a cigarette," he said, glad to have cigarettes in his pocket.

"I should have turned to the right. This path isn't on my course. I made a mistake. This is a cul-de-sac. If I keep going, it will lead me right into the arms of my pursuers. With my own two feet I brought myself here. Who confused me?" This alarm came too late. Fatigue gradually drew him into sleep as if with strong ropes.

In his sleep he was at home once again, at his mother's side. Before she was hospitalized in the sanatorium, a kind of marvelous efflorescence seized her. She would tell stories and describe things with well-chosen words and fitting adjectives. That's when he heard for the first time that in her youth the

Prince of Zauberberg had been in love with her and asked for her hand. The young prince even came to her parents' house. Her parents received his offer with pride. They even agreed that their daughter might convert, but the prince, who constantly competed in horse races, fell from his horse and broke his neck, never to rise again. That bitter news struck them all a hard blow. The parents dressed in mourning and wanted to attend the funeral. Their request was refused without explanation. Years passed, and the matter was forgotten by everyone. But it was not erased from his mother's heart. In the last months she talked about the prince as though he were a redeeming angel who would return and ask for her hand again.

In the last months she was lovely, with an attractive, frightening beauty. For hours he would sit by her side and listen to her. A new kind of melody was in her voice. In the sanatorium too she attracted special attention. The attendants who came to get her on occasion used to say, "Everyone is waiting for you."

"How is Doctor Weltsch?" she would inquire.

"He is in excellent health. He's already asked about you."

The short stays in the sanatorium were mysterious and hateful to him. Though he had visited her several times, her conduct there was cold and artificial. It was as though she wasn't his beloved mother but rather a stepmother. On returning from there she was all his, flourishing, talking with tempestuous enthusiasm and full freedom. Yet sometimes a kind of dread would seize her. Her eyes would change, and a kind of yellow spark would look out of them.

During one of her attacks she ordered him: "Go to Hofheim and see what they've done to the chapel."

"Now?"

"Right away. My heart tells me that a catastrophe has happened. One mustn't leave the place unattended."

He left the house. He didn't go to Hofheim, of course. Upon his return, two hours later, he told her everything was in its proper place. She looked at him distrustfully, which was unusual.

Between one vacation and another she talked about colors and fragrances and about a few scenes of her childhood. She spoke with a kind of stunning precision and without a hint of exaggeration. In his heart he already knew then that many people close to him would be erased from his memory, but not his mother. Every one of her movements, her arm on the arm of the chair, the way she passed her hand over her hair, the way she grasped her lipstick, the shoes with the high heels—all her gestures would live with him for many years. That would be his hidden joy. But sometimes a voice would cry out from within her with frightening savagery. She would sit and reprimand him accusingly. These, it seems, were old accounts, hidden and forgotten pains, that were aroused in her and demanded satisfaction.

At that time the attendants used to come and go like members of the family. Whenever he called for them, they would come. Seeing their peasantlike stature, she would quiet down and offer them a cold drink. She would say, "I'm going to change clothes. Wait a moment. I can't go out dressed like this. Meanwhile Theo will tell you about all the signs and wonders."

Sometimes they would sit for an hour and tell Theo jokes or banter about the nurses and doctors. Theo didn't know the staff well, but from their talk he learned that there too were loves and hates, and sometimes a prominent doctor would slip up and fall in love with one of his patients.

XII

WHEN HE WOKE UP his mother's face still fluttered before his eyes. The light was full, and he tried to dim the powerful concreteness of the night. Now he knew that at no great distance from there he would be trapped by the refugees. He was not afraid. A kind of quiet curiosity told him to sit, to light a cigarette, and to wait with patience. He enjoyed that expectation.

The morning light through the thick leaves was soft and chilly, bringing the sight of his hometown before his eyes, the way to high school, the tram, and the thin mist that would crawl at the foot of fences in the morning. Even then he had known, though dimly, that the hidden time would destroy many dear sights within him, but not the marvelous thin mist at the foot of the wooden fences. Even then he had known—and he was only fifteen years old—that the wild horses, harnessed to wild chariots, were about to storm them and destroy the thin skein he had spun over the years on the way home from high school. Sometimes on his return from school a clear and strong feeling would flood him and shut off his weary consciousness, making him mingle with the noise of the gardens. Once he told his mother some of this, but his mother was sunk in her own visions. She shook herself and said: "Just the little wooden churches, just chapels, I am moved. Only there do I wish to bend my knee."

When he finished high school and was on his way to Vienna—or, rather, on his way to Vienna to find out how he could get to Zurich and register at the university there—she said out loud: "You are going on your way. Don't forget to spread your wings. Remember your mother. There are many selfish women in the world. Don't pay attention to them. They are bad women. Spread your wings and take off to the gates of radiance. Music doesn't lie."

The next day, when he returned disappointed and fatigued, she met him with a festive voice: "How wonderful that you've returned to me. How could I have managed without you? It's good you listened to me."

The sight of the night and closeness to his mother strengthened him, and he strode without fear. The valley grew narrower, and the gentle slope pulled his feet along. He was pleased that fear no longer plagued him. He walked to his fate with head high.

At a bend in the trail he found an abandoned campfire. It seemed that the men had spent the night there and in the morning had gone on their way, leaving supplies and utensils. The breathing embers in the heart of that silent forest stunned him with their simplicity, and though he was thirsty, he did not rush to prepare a mug of coffee for himself. For a long while he stood and looked at that neglect as though marveling. While he was sitting there, mug in hand, he heard a clear voice: "Why did you push him hard?"

"I didn't push him hard, sir," he responded immediately.

"Don't call me sir. No irrelevant remarks. Did you use two hands or one?"

"I don't remember."

"Don't say you don't remember."

"One hand. My other hand was blocked."

"With your right or your left hand?"

"With my left hand."

"What did you tell him?"

"I told him I was about to convert to Christianity."

"To state a fact or to anger him?"

"To state a fact."

"Did you consider that such an idea was liable to drive him out of his mind?"

"His reaction was quiet, I would say, and relaxed."

"Then why did he attack you?"

"I don't know. At any rate, I pushed him lightly."

"We'll use instruments to measure how hard you pushed him. In a little while the instruments will come, and we'll check."

Theo woke up. The questions were clear, as if they had gone through a dense sieve. Evidently these were merely preliminary questions. The following questions would be more detailed, and he would have to answer them at length. Why, for example, had he left his friends and gone off on his own without saying good-bye to them? What harm had they done him in all those years? They used to divide their portion of bread equally, and when he fell ill with typhus they did his quota of work until he recovered. And after he recovered they gave him extra bread so he would get better.

It was clear to him that the following questions would touch on many matters, on loves and hates, his hostility toward the refugees. "Anyone who was in the camps deserves a lot of love. Without love, there can be no existence. We must be together. Together all the time." When had he heard those sentences? Who had spoken them? Now it seemed to him that a blind man had whispered it, one of the blind men who had managed to conceal their blindness from the soldiers.

When he knew what to expect, it was as if his desire to stand trial was fortified. Immediately, without knowing what he was doing, he said the following sentence: "I pushed him lightly. With one hand, with my palm. I didn't mean to knock him down."

"We heard that." The voice was speedy in coming.

"With one hand, with my palm."

"We heard that too."

"It wasn't a push so much as a pretext."

"What kind of pretext is he talking about?"

"Quiet. Bend your knee and beg forgiveness. If you have a spark of faith, bend your knee and beg forgiveness. Beg forgiveness from everyone who is walking or sitting next to the tree, and cry out: 'I have sinned, I have trespassed, I have transgressed.'" It wasn't a voice, it was a chorus of voices, flaring up all at once, and the fire let out a searing heat.

From then on he walked with no fear. Cans of sardines, flour, and candies were strewn by the sides of the road. The refugees rummaged through them, took a little, and left most of it. They even left full packs of cigarettes. "Let me at him."

He remembered the voice of his bunkmate Mendel Dorf. He was a plain man who liked other people with simple affection, and in the bitterest moments he never lost his faith in God. When people were sitting on their bunks and weeping like children, he would go to them softly and talk to them as though they were his children. He was thirty. Over the years in the camp his face changed completely and he looked like a man of fifty, but the light in his face never went out.

Theo remembered him now with a kind of sharpness, as though he were standing next to him. An unforgettable face, perhaps because there was nothing outstanding in it. He was religious, and because of his faith he suffered greatly. The other slave laborers didn't like the way he got up early, didn't like his prayers and benedictions. Even though his prayers were entirely inconspicuous, they made people angry at him. "Don't pray, don't recite blessings," they would hiss at him, as though he were doing something shameful in public. Physically he was a strong man, and he was capable of giving his tormenters as good as he got, but he never harmed a soul. He loved people with a submissive, annoying love, a love full of self-abnegation. "What stupidity, what hypocrisy," people would shout at him. They refused to see free will in his actions. Moreover, they were sure that he only did what he did to buy their hearts.

He helped many people, but few expressed gratitude. They took his simplicity for stupidity, his faith for a habit, and his help for self-interest. Theo didn't like him either, but in time, as he observed him, he changed his opinion somewhat.

One evening, while they were on their way home, the Ukrainians whipped them, and one of the prisoners collapsed. He was a large man, and it was hard to drag him. In their apathy they were about to abandon him. It was Mendel who took it upon himself to drag him along, and he brought him to the shed. The man didn't thank him, not even the next day.

"Why don't you thank Mendel?" someone dared to ask.

"It's hard for me to thank him."

"Forget about those habits. They drive people crazy. Is it so hard for you to understand that? After the war, in your room, you can pray to your heart's content. Just not here. This isn't the place for prayer. Those grimaces drive people crazy. Why provoke people?"

"I pray quietly."

"But you move. Stop that."

"I can't."

"You don't want to, that's the truth."

"The people will murder you, don't you understand?"

"What can I do?"

"Stop."

"But I have to."

"It's madness. There's no other word for it."

One morning a prisoner got up and hit him. The prayer had apparently driven him wild, and he attacked Mendel with all of his rage. Mendel seized his hands and begged, "Don't hit me."

"I'm going to kill you."

"What did I do to you?"

"You're driving me crazy."

If the other prisoners hadn't intervened he would have attacked Mendel again. Strange, no one condemned him for his wickedness, as though everyone agreed that Mendel's morning prayers were malicious. But the worst offense Mendel suffered came a few months before the liberation. One of the prisoners called to him, "Your behavior is a disgrace. For shame! That isn't Jewish behavior. It's Christian behavior, false behavior."

Mendel didn't reply to that insult either. He bore the humiliation in silence. His face had no prominent feature, so that you couldn't call it handsome or ugly. His face was round in its simplicity. Theo saw it now with a kind of clarity, as though Mendel were standing by his side.

XIII

NOW THE MORNING LIGHTS streamed through the gully. The sight reminded him of a narrow, stubborn brook, chased by the heights of winter. Theo's feet were light. Wandering over those deserted hillcrests removed burden after burden from his shoulders. Now his shoulders were left bare and free. If it weren't for the remaining scraps of fear, his feet would have glided along even more lightly. Those scraps gradually wafted away, and a kind of oblivion cushioned itself within him. "In another two weeks, two and a half weeks, I'll be home," his lips murmured distractedly.

That of course was an illusion. The gully grew narrower and narrower. The steep walls grew closer to each other, and green moisture filled the space until it was stifling. This difficulty didn't keep him from advancing. On the contrary, a strong emotion, such as he had felt before the liberation, told him that the end of his journey was approaching, and that he would do well to hurry his steps. That feeling was not idle. Before long the gully decanted into a green expanse, packed with thin tree trunks. At first the area looked unpopulated. But the sight became clear to him immediately. On the ground many refugees lay crowded together, with package upon package by their sides. The smell of coffee stood in the enclosed space. In the corners a few sloppy campfires burned, emitting a blinding smoke. If he had any doubt, the old, familiar words came and testified that here people battled over every bit of ground, were attentive to every word, and as sensitive to every expression as they had been in the notorious transit camps.

"I shouldn't have come here. This is a mistake. A dreadful mistake." He spoke without noticing that the words were leaving his mouth. For a moment he turned his head to see whether there was a way to retreat. The place was like a tent, but the exits were blocked by thin tree trunks.

"Where are you from and where are you going?" A voice came soon.

"Camp eight, on my way home." He was as sparing as possible with words. Nevertheless he added, "What's this here?"

"A transit camp," a woman answered matter-of-factly.

"Transit to where?"

"I don't know," she said, spreading her arms.

Theo halted his feet. The light spotted the people's faces with a kind of thick greenness, as though they came from some unknown region of life.

"How do you get out of here?" he asked.

"You can get out from there." The woman pointed at a small passage, where many people had crowded together with their bundles. There was no noise and no shouting, which only augmented the impression made by the green light.

"How long have you been here?"

"Two weeks now."

"I made a mistake. I shouldn't have come here. Believe me, I shouldn't have come here," he mumbled.

The woman and two other women sitting at her side absorbed his words in silence. "Still, how is it that you got here?" the woman asked in a voice that sounded annoying.

"I was on my way to my hometown. I apparently didn't stick to the course. That shaded gully tempted me, and I got off course."

"We didn't intend to get here either," she said, and a sigh such as he hadn't heard for a long time escaped from her breast.

A few people were sprawled on their bundles. The bundles were long and round and didn't look like belongings so much as parts of bodies that were mingled with the living limbs. That combination added a kind of strength to their sprawl. It was clear they were prepared for anything. Nothing would surprise them again. They looked at the people near the passage with apathetic contempt. Theo knew that apathy intimately, but here, in this narrow space, it had reached fulfillment.

"May I offer you a mug of coffee?" the woman said and turned her head toward her friends as though asking their consent.

"Gladly, I'm very thirsty. There are plenty of supplies here, I see. We won't die of hunger." Loquacity was restored to him.

"There's more than enough here. People are going crazy."

"What's going on here?"

"What isn't going on here?" the woman answered in the old-fashioned Jewish way.

"It's disorderly, I assume." Theo found that unexceptional phrase and used it.

"Disorderly, you say. There are dangerous rapists here. You can't sleep at night. A rapist bit me here on the leg," the woman's friend said and exposed her leg to show him.

"It's a dark place." Theo summed up for himself.

Close by a few men sat playing poker. The thin expression on their faces bespoke tension and concentration. The cards were thrown down with gestures of self-assurance and provocation. Their fingers, perhaps because of the green light, looked very sharp. "I won't stay here long." The sentence escaped Theo's mouth. That was a sentence people used to say in the camp at various times and in various tones. Astonishingly it had now fallen into Theo's mouth as well. "Why did you women come here?"

"We walked with all the others."

"One mustn't walk with all the others," he was going to answer the woman, but seeing her face, a good, anguished face, he restrained himself. Not far away sat a few young women, laughing out loud. There was much closeness among them, and they didn't need to use words, just syllables. It had been years since he'd heard such open laughter.

"I made a mistake." Theo raised his voice again. "That gully tempted me. True, it's easier to advance in a green gully than to climb over bare hillcrests. But the advantage of hillcrests is immeasurable. On a hillcrest you're a free man."

"What difference does it make?" the woman said in a voice whose shadings Theo knew well.

"It makes a big difference. If I had walked on the hillcrests, I wouldn't have ended up here. The hillcrest is where you move freely. On a hillcrest you're a free man."

"Are you sure?"

"I have no doubt. This togetherness brings only disaster. Anyone can come and block up this valley. We must scatter, walk on the hillcrests, and the sooner the better for us. Anywhere but here."

"Don't talk so loudly."

"Why?"

"There are people here who are of a different opinion."

"The war is over. One is allowed to speak."

"You may be right, but there are people here who constantly eavesdrop. They are sensitive to words, to opinions and beliefs." As she spoke the woman prepared a sandwich and served it to him the way one serves a person one is close to, without ceremony. The sandwich was filled with sardines and pickled cucumbers. The black bread and the sour cucumber brought the smell of a country inn to his nostrils, where the odors are pungent and everything is served from big barrels bound with thick hoops.

The silence was disturbed all at once. At some distance from the tree trunks, bound in thin ropes, three short, thin men were being led along. They walked together, crammed up against each other. "Have pity on us, Jews, have pity on us. We didn't do a thing," they begged. The guards behind them didn't prod them along or silence them. None of the people lying there asked what was their sin or crime. The prisoners advanced, leaning on each other.

"Who are they?" asked Theo.

"The informers. Don't you know?" the woman answered matter-of-factly. The two women sitting at her side smiled involuntarily.

"We are commanded to help one another, not abuse each other," a voice simpered within him. Theo knew that these women were doing the right thing at that time, without asking for any reward for themselves. In the end the prisoners weren't so righteous, and a little disgrace wouldn't do them any harm.

The prisoners were led to a deep trench. They realized that would be their place from now on, and they stood still. The guards received mugs of coffee, and they sat and drank. The expression on their faces was quiet and impassive.

"Where did you find them?" someone asked loudly.

"They came by themselves," the guard answered curtly.

"You're not giving us anything to drink? Aren't we human beings?" One of the prisoners addressed the people sprawling all around them.

"Informers don't deserve anything." A voice was heard.

"There is no God in your heart," the prisoner answered in old-fashioned words.

No one responded. The clearing was drenched in green and shady light; the earth was soaked with moisture, and people lay on their bundles or on boxes, on which the word "Ammunition" was written in German.

Later one of the prisoners asked the guard, "What do you intend to do to us?"

"Why should I tell you?" the guard answered without looking at him.

"We're human beings, not beasts of the field."

"Informers aren't human beings."

"Will they have a trial?"

"Don't be so curious. Everything will be clear to you soon enough."

One of the women approached the pit and handed them mugs of coffee. The prisoners grasped the mugs with trembling hands and in their great avidity they forgot to thank her. No one made any remark. The prisoners drank in long gulps and without exchanging a word among themselves.

As always on such occasions, Theo felt a crude pleasure because it was they, not he, standing in the trench; he was not the accused who would have to face trial. He knew it was a crude feeling, but nevertheless he felt relieved. For a moment he thought of addressing the women and thanking them. But he immediately saw the stupidity of that desire.

In one corner people were carousing, drinking vodka and singing dirty songs. Their reddened faces looked wicked, expressing malicious joy and stupidity: "They're informers, they deserve what they get." The prisoners in the trench didn't respond. Their hatless heads looked more spiritual than those about them. Perhaps it was because their jaws weren't grinding food.

"Are you planning to kill us?" asked one of the prisoners, who could no longer restrain himself.

"Everything will be clear to you soon enough," answered a guard without looking at him.

"Even the Germans treated us with more mercy."

"Don't talk. You'd better not talk," the guard answered with feigned nonchalance.

The three prisoners sat on the bottom of the trench and looked more like smugglers than collaborators. They were thin, unshaven, and a kind of bitterness dripped from their lips. Now it seemed they weren't hostile to the guards but to their fellow prisoners in the trench. One of them rolled up his pant leg and nervously scratched at a wound that had scabbed over.

"What are they planning to do to them?" Theo asked.

"They'll whip them," the woman answered matter-of-factly.

"That's what they do all the time here?"

"Yes."

"Where did they catch them?"

"In the pass."

This short conversation darkened his spirit. In his embarrassment he held out his mug and said, "If you would kindly pour me some more coffee, I would be very grateful." That soft and courteous appeal brought a smile to the woman's face. It had apparently been years since anyone had used words like that to her.

"I'll make you another sandwich. I can see you're hungry," she said in a full, motherly voice.

Afterward people threw cans of sardines and biscuits into the trench. The prisoners gathered the food without fighting among themselves. They did it with long, animal-like movements. They immediately squatted down and ate without a word. Their appetite was visible. Everyone could tell they had nothing in the world now except what was thrown to them. All their being was concentrated on eating.

For a long time the prisoners squatted and chewed the food that had been thrown to them. Every once in a while one of the crowd would make some remark to them, but no one harmed them. The guards sat by the trench and observed them. Their eyes were tense like the eyes of cattle dealers.

"They have to be taught a lesson." An elderly man approached the guard.

"Don't worry. We'll teach them," the guard answered him out loud.

"We've suffered because of them," said the elderly man, returning to his place.

The woman handed Theo another sandwich and asked: "Where do you intend to go?" The word "intend" stung Theo's ear for a moment, and he quickly replied, "Home. Hasn't the time come to return home?" He pronounced the word "home" with a strange emphasis, as though he were trying to regain possession of something that had been wrested away from him by force.

"Where is your home, if I may ask?" the woman inquired with old-fashioned courtesy.

"Baden-bei-Wien."

"A pretty town, everyone says." The woman again used a familiar expression. She apparently wished to add something but restrained herself.

"In two weeks I'll get home. It's no more than three hundred fifty miles away."

"I won't go home. I'll never go home. Anyplace is my home, just not there."

"From now on you'll be homeless, always on the road, always with the refugees?" he asked in a needling way.

"The company of the refugees is more pleasant to me than that of the murderers."

"We're exaggerating a little, aren't we?" He used that strange way of speaking.

"Correct, we exaggerate purposely, to make things visible. Hasn't the time come for things to appear in black and white and in relief?"

Now Theo knew that the woman was educated. She had certainly studied at a university, graduated, and worked as a teaching assistant. She had written some papers that had caused a stir. For some reason he imagined her sitting in an armchair, surrounded by books and journals. For a moment he wanted to ask her about the institution where she had taught, the registration period, and the fees. But he restrained himself and returned to his subject: "Always together. Always with those informers."

"That's true."

"And you won't go back home?"

"Never."

The two women sitting next to her did not enter the conversation. It was hard to tell from their faces whether they agreed or disagreed with what she was saying. The expression of their faces was frozen, as though they were sunk in a kind of prolonged astonishment.

The woman added: "I love every one of them. I learned to love them: it was hard for me to love them. But now they are dear to me. I can sit for hours and listen to everything that happened to them. They don't always want to talk. But I learned to listen to them."

"Aren't you frightened?"

"Why be afraid? Every refugee is a precious person. I can no longer live in the world of pleasures. Do you understand?"

In the meantime the guards got to their feet. At first glance it seemed they were stretching their upper limbs, and that they would sit down again. But that was not their intention. Without warning or ceremony they raised their staffs and whirled them down on the backs of the prisoners. The prisoners were taken by surprise and lay on the ground as if during a bombing. But they immediately got up and swiftly fled to the corners. They didn't shout but sobbed, a sob of fear and helplessness. They raced about on all fours, running away from the staves that pursued them.

"Have pity, Jews. Why are you standing by?" one of them raised his head and implored the people around him. No one responded.

"Informers must be beaten mercilessly." One of the crowd finally found some words to strengthen the hands of the beaters. They were beating, but without pleasure. Their expression was one of disgust, contempt, and strange anger.

"Aren't you ashamed to ask for pity?" The guard brought his staff down on one of the prisoners' legs. It wasn't a heavy blow, but very painful. The prisoner emitted a kind of unpleasant gurgle, the grunt of an animal.

"Informers shall have no reprieve." The guard kept hitting him without pausing.

"Kill us, don't torture us." One of them begged for death. But that request received no response. They continued beating them, in disorganized fashion, which made the punishment cruel and ugly. Finally the guards wearied, put their staffs down on the ground, and sat down next to them. The prisoners still kept sobbing, an imploring sob. They were afraid the dreadful barrage would resume.

No one in the crowd heckled them anymore, and no one asked for revenge. The beaters squatted and sipped coffee in leisurely fashion. Their faces revealed nothing. They sat where they were, as though they had done their duty. Near them a few men sat and played cards avidly. Nothing happening around them, not even the public punishment of the informers, was of interest to them. Sweat poured down their faces as though it were summer.

Before long the informers were forgotten. Other sounds, squabbles and laughter, filled the valley. An elderly man, of impressive stature and height, raised his arms and let out an old-fashioned, heart-rending "Oy" from deep in his chest, and for a moment it made the fragile silence quake with fright.

"Can I leave here now?" Theo asked.

"Of course. Why are you asking?"

"It seemed to me that while they were carrying out the sentence, they blocked all the exits."

"They didn't close them. Everything is open. It just looked that way to you." The woman spoke in a conciliatory and slightly annoying manner.

"I was mistaken. Everything is open, you say?"

"Why are you in a hurry? It's hard to understand why you're in such a hurry," the woman said clearly.

"I'm returning home. The time has come to detach myself from all this hubbub. For three years I was punished for no crime at all. Now the time has come to get out of here. I have no reason to stay here." He meant to speak these explicit words, but, maddeningly, they stuck in his throat.

The woman absorbed that muteness, turned her head back to see whether anyone was around, and when she was certain there was no one, she said: "Why are you doing this to yourself? No one is guilty, not even the informers. You'll never be able to return home. Our houses have been destroyed forever. That loss can never be restored."

"I'm going home because I love my home," Theo answered irrelevantly.

"Why be stubborn?" she said. The women sitting at his side were listening intently all the time. She added: "I, at any rate, wouldn't be in such a hurry. There are ruins and spirits everywhere. Why go back and meet them face to face? Forgive me if I tell you this. It's hard for me to hide my feelings from you."

"My mother"—Theo spoke with a strange kind of seriousness—"loved Baden-bei-Wien, the churches and chapels. She was a native. In so many words. At one time she wanted to convert, but my father, because of some principle that isn't clear to me, refused, although he too had a positive attitude toward church music. My mother spent days on end in churches. Excuse me for telling you personal things. I myself, how shall I say it, I had no connection at all to the Jewish faith. It's distant and strange to me."

The words which Theo spoke sounded too loud. The two other women next to the woman he was talking to raised their heads. It was evident that his words had frightened them.

"I don't know what to say to you," said the woman, spreading out her hands.

"I didn't want to hide anything from you," said Theo. "If I went away without telling you the truth, I would feel as though I had defrauded you."

"Your desire to return home is entirely understandable to me. It's an illusion, a dreadful illusion. We have no home anymore. We no longer have anything. I'm not a religious woman, but to convert to Christianity now seems to me like suicide. It's hard for me to explain that to you. I, at any rate, wouldn't do it for any price in the world."

"Forgive me." He wanted to avoid hurting her feelings.

"How can I explain it, my dear? It's as though you took me

back to the camp. As if you asked me to speak Ukrainian. As if you'd ripped my body to shreds. That thought causes me no pain, just disgust."

"I'm afraid to talk with him." The woman sitting beside the speaker was roused from her thoughts.

"Why? What harm have I done?"

"He frightens me," said the woman, with a terrified face.

"I"—Theo raised his voice—"didn't mislead you. I revealed my intentions to you. The truth itself."

"He frightens me," the woman repeated with a trembling voice.

"Don't tell anyone your intentions. If they learn about your intention here, they'll give you a beating. Keep quiet and don't be stubborn. Do whatever you want, but not here. Here you mustn't express such opinions." There was something frighteningly motherly in her voice.

Now, with great clarity, Theo remembered the fateful push that had moved that sturdy man from his place, his fall, and the powerful groan that had escaped from his throat. It was clear to him now as well that it wasn't a hard push, but apparently a very effective one, because the man fell down immediately. Theo's hand didn't hurt, just a kind of chill that spread over his entire body. It was somewhat stranger than the chill that spread over his fingers now. Theo rose to his feet and said, "I'm going."

"Farewell," said the woman. "Don't talk with people too much. There are thoughts that shouldn't be expressed, even to yourself. Surely you know that."

Theo now turned toward the shallow trench where the informers lay with their legs extended, looking comfortable. If it weren't for the bloodstains on their torn clothing, one couldn't have known they were beaten. Their manner of sitting showed patience and stupidity. For a moment he stood and looked at them from close by. The closeness excited him, but he didn't dare go down and talk to them. "Be well," he finally said. The informers raised their eyes without responding.

Theo turned in the direction of the ravine that shed long shadows on the people's faces. The people lay at ease next to tree trunks. The few words that were spoken were familiar. Next to one of the tree trunks sat a short man, wrapped in shadows, and if it weren't for his mumbling lips, one wouldn't notice his existence at all. "Why am I sitting here?" he murmured. "Why don't I move along? I'm falling behind. I'm losing precious time. I've already lost more than enough." Theo absorbed the full force of that voice and approached the man.

"Where do you have to go?" Theo asked as if he had a vehicle at his disposal.

"I have to get to the university," the man answered seriously. "I've lost two full years. If I'm not there on time, I'll also lose the third year. In two weeks the registration closes. Do you understand me?"

"Don't worry. You'll get there on time. Usually they extend the registration period."

"I see you're familiar with this. Where are you from? I have to get to Budapest, and I'm being detained here for no reason at all. It's a good thing I met you. It's good to have someone to consult with."

"Why don't you set out?" Theo spoke in the voice of former times.

"Something within me won't let me go. I'm frightened.

Because of this fear I'm held back here, stuck in this place. Every day, the same sight: every day they beat the informers in the trench. It's unbearable by now."

"You have to overcome your fear."

"True, you're right."

"You should get up and go. Walking dissipates fear. You can make fifteen miles a day without forcing yourself. And it's good to walk on the hillcrests, the hillcrests are open, the view is broad. Don't go down into the valley. Disasters of every kind swarm in the valleys. The hillcrests are safe places. Within two or three weeks you'll get to Budapest."

"Are you sure?" A spark lit up in the man's eyes.

"Beyond any doubt."

"Thank you," said the man. "I'll do it immediately. It's good I met you. If it weren't for you, I'd be sitting here forever. I'm ashamed to tell you. Something in me isn't right. But now I won't give in again. I promise you," he said, getting to his feet and turning away.

XIV

THEO LEFT THE RAVINE and immediately climbed up to the hillcrest. The blue lights of the evening were spread out on the plain. The weeds beneath his feet were green and thick, but not wet. He advanced with ease, as though his legs had been freed from shackles.

From here he could see the valley, wrapped in trees and echoing with the rumble of running water. There were no birds to be seen, but from time to time a thin, frightening whine would filter up from there. In Theo's head a kind of wakefulness gradually opened up, a bright awareness. It was as if the curtains of the heavens had been stretched and he himself were raised up and saw the long, winding road at his feet, since he had left his fellows and the gates of the camp: the entire course along the valleys and hilltops, the tree trunks, the crates, the containers, the cartons, the coffee and cigarettes. It was clear to him that everything had happened just a month ago, but in his soul the time was far longer. As he stood his face came back to life. With great clarity he saw Mendel Dorf, wrapped in a prayer shawl, wearing phylacteries, standing motionless, as though the prayer had mummified him. "Mendel," he wanted to call to him, "why are you turning your back on me?" But he immediately understood that Mendel could no longer move. He and his prayer had become one. From then on no one would harm him. And Theo too felt a kind of relief in his body, the kind one feels after an extended effort. He was pleased to have extricated himself from the valley and from the people lying there. The woman's face was erased from his memory, but the young men in the shallow trench still stood before his eyes. Their long, sooty arms, stretched out to the cans of sardines, the way they had bitten and chewed. The way they had sat motionless.

Evening fell suddenly and arched over his head. The blue colors changed shade, and space narrowed to a dark tunnel that steadily closed in on him. For a moment he wanted to get out of it, but it was too late. He bent over. Immediately the face appeared to him again, a clear face, washed over with astonishment. All those who had witnessed the murder. He also saw the victim. He woke from his faint and asked, "Do you intend to return to your hometown?"

"I do."

"Why are you going to convert to Christianity? All the blood within me is boiling. I'm not religious, but the thought that you're going to convert to Christianity saws through my flesh. I don't know how to explain that to you. But you're intelligent, and you understand the difference between thought and sawing."

"I'm going to the place where Bach dwells. The place where Bach dwells is like a temple. I have no other place in the world. Now I'm making a pilgrimage to him."

"It's wickedness. Greater wickedness than that would be hard to describe. I'm not a religious man, but the thought that you're going back to your hometown to convert to Christianity makes me into a primordial Jew."

"You can't stop me even if you cut off my legs."

"You'll never get there," the man said and fell down the way he had fallen when Theo pushed him.

That night Theo slept in an open field, a sleep without visions or dreams. He was with his body as he had not been since the war. The darkness bundled him, and he wasn't cold.

When he awoke the next morning he wasn't sure if he had really acted right with all the people he had met on his long way. In fact, they hadn't asked for anything. They only wanted to give him things. But he had arrogantly ignored the frightened, outstretched hands. Not even a single word of gratitude.

Now he knew that something in him had gone wrong. For example, the hostility to Yiddish. Only toward the liberation had he known clearly that his accent had been ruined, and that he would have to work hard in order to restore the correct intonation to his expression. Then for the first time he felt that something within him had gone awry. When he left the camp and set out, he had only wanted to uproot from within him the words that had stuck to him. Words like "toytn" and "lemekh." He knew that if he met his mother, she would scold him for using the foreign words that had clung to him. His mother was sensitive to words, to choice, to the correct order. Even in the rabbinical divorce court she had tried to correct the rabbis' German, making the chief justice of the tribunal angry. He had shouted: "This is not the academy of the German language but a divorce court. One does not, madam, correct a rabbi's language. We will be accepted in the world to come even without German grammar."

His father had also been punctilious about proper language, but it was a different kind of insistence: on syntactical precision. Now he knew that the language had escaped him. The Yiddish of the camps had done it in. From now on he would speak only the Yiddish of the camps. That fear, that his mother had planted in him from the time he was nursing, filled him again.

These thoughts held him back, but he recovered and advanced. The path was narrow, only a trail. Deserted meadows extended for many miles. Animals were missing from that whole tranquil vista, and that made the silence a lie.

"Coffee, a cup of coffee." The words escaped his mouth in his mother's voice. His mother's words always inspired him with the will to live. A strong kind of vitality was drawn out of them. In fact it wasn't German but a language of her own that sounded like German. People had trouble understanding it. But for him it was an open and entertaining language. Coffee, a cup of coffee, what could be simpler than that? But she expressed those simple words in a way that no one else could express them.

"What is she saying?" they would sometimes ask him in the sanatorium."

"My mother is asking you to dim the light. The light is too harsh." That was true. That was her intention.

He advanced. There was no one in that barren expanse,

just meadows. The emptiness surrounded him on all sides
and inspired him with fear, the fear of being left alone and
without cigarettes. The cigarettes were running low, and that
occupied his thoughts. Since the war was over it had been
hard for him to be without cigarettes.

"At the inn I'll buy cigarettes," he said for some reason. But
that distraction brought the image of his mother's face before
his eyes. It wasn't his mother from years ago, but the one who
had gone to her fate alone, dressed in a fur coat and a fur hat
and with high-heeled shoes. Who had greeted her at the
train? She had gone to her fate without a knapsack or bundle,
the way one goes to the theater. It occurred to him that as she
stood in the doorway of the railroad car, coarsely crammed
in, she had said in that voice of hers, "I don't like this hurly-
burly." That was the sentence. That and no other. He was
glad he had finally found the sentence she had uttered at the
edge of the abyss.

While he was standing in that thick silence he discovered a
shed on the horizon. It was a long shed that immediately
reminded him of the long sheds in the camp. Two months
before the defeat they had added eight more sheds. Everyone
was sure they were going to bring new slave laborers. That was
a vain fear. The defeat was absolute, and anyone left alive
picked up his feet and set out. The thought that there might
be refugees there drove him to the side, but he was tired and
thirsty and had already gone two days without coffee and
cigarettes. So he decided, "Come what may."

The horizon turned out not to be far away. On the rib of the
mountain a low shed stood, of the kind the Germans built
next to workshops. As he drew near it seemed to him that the
shed was full of refugees, and he immediately wanted to

withdraw. This time he was mistaken, but not completely. Six refugees, four men and two women, lay in a corner.

"Who's there?" Theo called out.

"Who are you looking for?"

"I'm mistaken," he said and turned aside.

"Come in. We have coffee and cigarettes."

"I don't want to waste the time."

"Just one mug. We won't hold you up."

They sat on the ground, still dressed in prisoner's uniforms, surrounded by boxes. The light penetrating through the cracks in the shed lit their faces a little. He had no desire to sit in their company, and he turned his back on them.

"Why do you look down on us?" a man called out in a strident voice. "Believe me, we never harmed anyone. We may not be righteous men, but we're not contemptible. We suffered enough in the camps."

"What do you want from me?" Theo spoke to him, trembling.

"Why do you look down on us? You were in a camp too, and you know that we couldn't behave any differently. Other people may not understand that, but you were in the camps. You mustn't look down on us. Among us are martyrs for the sake of man. That mute man there, sitting at my side, used to give his meager crust to two sick people. You mustn't look down on him."

"I don't look down on him."

"So why are you running away from us? We mustn't run away and leave behind the sick and weak. You should take one of the sick people and bring him to a safe place. We aren't like murderers."

"I'm going home," Theo shouted as though talking to a deaf man.

"You know very well that no one is waiting for us at home. Take one of the sick people and bring him to a safe place. That will be your reward."

"What did I do to you? Why are you tormenting me?"

"Pardon me. I didn't mean to torment you. I was speaking to you as to a brother. So very few have remained alive. In my camp there were only three, only three. There were a hundred and twenty-four of us, healthy, sound men, working at every kind of job. The winter was our undoing. If it weren't for the winter, more of us would be left. Only three are left. Do you get it?"

Now Theo saw what he had never seen in all that time: he and his father in one row; in front of them, the old Sachs brothers; and behind them Mr. and Mrs. Siegelbaum. Six in all. Surrounded by a mass of policemen. They left the police building and walked down Stifter Street, a shady street. At the windows women and children stood and watched their progress in silence. No one called out, no one opened his mouth. They walked in a seemingly aimless procession. The silence of autumn hung in the air. At the end of the street a paint contractor called out, "Death to the Jews, death to the merchants!" The synagogue, already abandoned, without worshipers for years, was gripped by flames at that moment. It burned quietly, without endangering the neighboring buildings.

On Schimmer Street a few women stood on a balcony, and a kind of malicious glee dripped from their eyes. The old man who walked in front of them stumbled and fell, but he recovered, stood up, and continued walking. When they neared the railroad station a worker came and slapped Mrs. Siegelbaum's face. Mrs. Siegelbaum fell to her knees, as though she were about to cross herself, and that strange sight aroused the laughter of the people around them.

From there to the railroad station the way was not long. At the entrance to the station they were ordered to get down on their knees. They crawled slowly, but without stumbling. In the courtyard a policeman ordered: "Now pray."

"We aren't religious. We don't know how to pray." His father spoke.

"So, you're heretics."

"We're not religious."

"You crooks," said the policeman and kicked him.

Afterward the policemen entered the buffet and quenched their thirst with beer. From time to time one of them would come out and shout, "Pray, heretics!" The lights of nighttime gradually faded, and a moist frost covered the square. The old men trembled with cold. At last, toward morning, a train stopped, and they were ordered to crawl into it.

"What are you thinking about?"

"Nothing," said Theo.

"There are some weak people among us whom we mustn't abandon now. We haven't lost the semblance of humanity. We must do what is incumbent upon us. Isn't that so?"

"What has to be done?" Theo asked voicelessly.

"To encourage them. If we don't watch over them, who will?" The man's voice had a kind of annoying insistence, as though he had rehearsed those lines. "I am not a religious man, and I shall probably never be one, but I feel that if we don't stretch out our hands, we are like murderers."

"I agree with you," said Theo, simply in order to silence his voice. However that very agreement aroused the man to speak more, and he continued talking about the need to stretch out one's hand, about the miserable brethren scattered on the deserted roads, about obligation and responsibility.

These open and simple words did indeed penetrate Theo's head, but they didn't shock him.

At that time it became clear to Theo beyond any doubt that he would never return to his hometown. From now on he would advance with the refugees. That language which his mother had inculcated in him with such love would be lost forever. If he spoke, he would speak only in the language of the camps. That clear knowledge made him dreadfully sad.

"What are you thinking about?" The man disturbed him again.

"Nothing."

"Thought is forbidden to us. Thought drives one mad. We must do as much good as possible." There was something clear and clean in the man's words, but nevertheless it wasn't pleasant.

"What must I do?" Theo asked in the tones of a prisoner.

"Sit for a moment and drink a mug of coffee. We'll make you a sandwich. You haven't drunk for a few days. A person has to drink. Without drinking, we'll collapse. How many days have you been on the road?"

"More than a month now, it seems to me."

"They liberated us on August fifteenth. Exactly two months ago. The man sitting by your side is mute. He became mute from the cold, but he can hear and understand. His name is Heinrich."

Theo bowed his head, as if at the sight of an amputated hand.

"Where did you intend to go?"

"To my hometown, to Baden-bei-Wien."

"There's no reason to go there. Stay here. We have everything we need. The shed is full of supplies. There's no sense seeking something that can never be attained. We won't bring the dead back to life. You understand that. Here we're together. I won't conceal from you that it isn't always comfortable, but still, we're together."

Theo gulped down mug after mug. The hot liquid seeped into him and filled him with warmth. Fatigue and helplessness assailed him. He placed his head on a bundle, curled up as if after a big quarrel, a desperate quarrel, closed his eyes, and collapsed.